TREASURY

A Collection of Favorite Stories
and Poems from Under the Sea

Disney's THE✿LITTLE MERMAID
TREASURY

A Collection of Favorite Stories and Poems from Under the Sea

DISNEY PRESS

NEW YORK

Printed in the United States of America.

First Edition
1 3 5 7 9 10 8 6 4 2

Library of Congress Catalog Card Number: 97-80154
ISBN: 0-7868-3182-0

CONTENTS

DISNEY's
THE ✦ LITTLE
MERMAID

The Complete Story

Adapted from the film by *A. L. Singer*

Black-and-white line drawings by *Philo Barnhart*

Paintings by *Ron Dias*

CHAPTER ONE

eave-ho!" The crew aboard the fine three-masted ship grunted as they pulled up a net filled with fish. It was all in a hard day's work at sea.

A young prince named Eric stood at the railing and lifted his face to the sea air. His faithful sheepdog, Max, stood by his side. The salty wind brushed back Eric's dark hair, and he smiled. The sea was his first love, and he could think of no better place to spend his birthday.

Eric gazed up into the thick clouds. "Isn't this great?" he said. "The salty sea air, the wind blowing in your face. A perfect day to be at sea!"

Near Eric, a gangly older man was bent over the railing. Slowly he raised himself. "Oh, yes," he said, his face green with seasickness. "Delightful." With a groan, he leaned over the side again.

Eric chuckled to himself. Old Grimsby had been his manservant for years, but he had never developed his sea legs.

"A fine strong wind and a following sea!" a sailor called out. "King Triton must be in a friendly mood."

"King Triton?" Eric asked, rushing over to help tie down a sail.

A crusty sailor named Sea Dog piped up, "Why, he's ruler of the merpeople, lad. Thought every good sailor knew about him."

"Hmph! Merpeople!" Grimsby said. "Eric, pay no attention to this nautical nonsense."

Sea Dog frowned. "But it ain't nonsense," he insisted, shaking a fish in Grimsby's face. "It's the truth! They're half fish and half human. I'm telling you, they live down in the depths of the ocean."

Eric had heard this argument many times before. Sea Dog and some of the other sailors were convinced that mer-people existed. Grimsby was absolutely certain they did

not. As for Eric, well, he simply didn't know what to think.

But if Eric could see to the bottom of the ocean, then he would know *exactly* what to think. For there, fathoms below Eric's ship, was the bustling kingdom of Atlantia. Merpeople and all the other creatures of the deep lived there—far away from human eyes—in a world all their own, a world presided over by the just and noble King Triton.

And on this very day, the entire kingdom had gathered to see the King's daughters sing in concert.

King Triton arrived at the concert hall in a golden chariot pulled by dolphins. His subjects cheered wildly. Soon after, a small crab appeared on a seashell pulled by goldfish. This was Sebastian, the royal court composer.

"I'm really looking forward to this performance, Sebastian," King Triton called out.

"Your Majesty," Sebastian replied, "this will be the finest concert I've ever conducted. Your daughters will be spectacular!"

"Yes," King Triton agreed. "And especially my little Ariel."

The King loved all his daughters. Each was a beauty and a great talent. But when it came to singing, Ariel outshone them all. Fish, crabs, sharks, clams—all the living things in the sea would stop to listen. Even the coral was said to sigh with pleasure at the sound of Ariel's singing.

"Ah, Ariel has the most beautiful voice!" Sebastian agreed. But as he rode toward the podium, he grumbled to himself, "If only she'd show up for rehearsals once in a while."

Ariel always seemed to have something better to do than attend her music lessons. And when she did show up, she was late more often than not. But with a big apology, a winning smile, *and* her lovely voice, it was hard for Sebastian to stay angry at her. As for where she had been keeping herself, nobody knew.

Sebastian climbed the podium. When he raised his baton, an orchestra of fish musicians lifted their instruments. An octopus drummer became poised with his drumsticks.

Down came the baton, and the musicians began to play. A curtain of bubbles rose upward. Three huge clamshells appeared on the stage. They opened to reveal six mermaids, all daughters of King Triton—Aquata, Andrina, Arista, Attina, Adella, and Alana.

As they swam around, singing sweetly, another closed clamshell swirled onto the stage. Everyone knew that Ariel was inside—and they couldn't wait to hear her sing.

Slowly, with all eyes upon it, the shell opened, and there, in the middle, stood…no one. The shell was empty.

The sisters stopped singing. Sebastian dropped his baton. The audience gasped in shocked surprise.

King Triton rose from his seat, clenching his trident. His face turned red with fury as he let out a bellow that shook the seafloor.

"Ariel!"

CHAPTER TWO

Ariel glided through the water at top speed. With each tail stroke, her red hair swept back like a thick flame. In her right hand she clutched a sturdy, empty sack. In a few minutes the sack would be filled with fascinating things—things from the world above the water. She couldn't wait.

Ariel stopped swimming when she reached an old shipwreck. The ship's rotting hull was covered with seaweed and barnacles, and the mast was broken in two. Through the portholes Ariel could see a glimpse of the dark and eerie interior.

To Ariel this was the most beautiful sight in the sea. A shipwreck was mysterious, exotic. It was from that *other* world.

Merpeople were forbidden to go above the water. It was King Triton's strictest rule—and one that Ariel just could not obey. Whenever she could, Ariel would sneak up to the surface to look around. She'd even made friends with a sea gull named Scuttle.

Ariel was curious about everything above the surface, especially the land creatures called humans. She knew her father's rule was designed to keep his subjects—including his daughters—from interacting with humans. King Triton said that these land creatures were dangerous and could not be trusted. Ariel had never seen any humans up close before, but she didn't understand how, if they could make all the beautiful things she had collected from the ocean floor, they could be so evil.

"Isn't this ship fantastic?" Ariel called over her shoulder.

"Yeah, sure," answered a small roly-poly fish, huffing and puffing to keep up with her. His name was Flounder, and he was Ariel's best friend.

He was not only terribly out of breath, he was scared, too.

"Uh, let's get out of here, Ariel," Flounder said. "It looks damp in there. And I think I may be coming down with a cough."

"Well, I'm going inside," Ariel said. "You can just stay here and watch for sharks."

Ariel swam through a porthole. "Sharks?" Flounder squeaked. *"Ariel, wait!"*

Flipping his fins wildly, Flounder headed right into the porthole—and got stuck. "Ariel, help!" he called out, twisting himself right and left.

Inside the ship, at the top of a staircase, Ariel turned. "Oh, Flounder...." Laughing, she swam back toward him.

Flounder shook with fear. "Ariel," he whispered, "do you really think there might be sharks around here?"

"Flounder, don't be such a guppy," Ariel said.

"I'm not a guppy!"

Thoonk! With a strong yank, Ariel pulled her friend into the ship.

Flounder stayed close to Ariel. The darkness frightened him. In every corner he saw strange, shadowy shapes. And he had an uneasy feeling that he and Ariel were being watched.

Ariel and Flounder swam up, through a hole in the ceiling, to the next level of the ship. There, on a pile of broken boards, lay a shiny, dented fork. Ariel gasped with delight and quickly swam over to seize it.

"Flounder," she sighed, "have you ever seen anything so wonderful in your life?"

"Wow! Cool!" Flounder said. "But what is it?"

"I don't know," Ariel said. "But I bet Scuttle will!"

Rrrrrrommm! Flounder jumped at the sound. Something had sped by the ship, something very large.

"What was that noise?" Flounder asked.

But Ariel was busy examining a curved tobacco pipe. "Hmm, I wonder what *this* is...."

Flounder turned to look behind him. A pair of angry yellow eyes stared in at him through a large window.

Below the eyes was a mouth filled with razor-sharp teeth.

"A shark!" Flounder shrieked. "Ariel, swim!"

CRRRRRAAASSSSSH! With a mighty thrust, the shark burst through the window, his jaws gaping wide.

Flounder sped off. With a loud *wham*, the shark's jaws clamped shut. Flounder could feel the water ripple behind him.

Ariel quickly threw the pipe into her sack. She and Flounder darted up to the next floor. They raced away, over broken wooden planks that jutted up from below.

Suddenly Ariel felt herself being jerked backward. She looked down in horror.

Her bag was stuck on a plank. Quickly she grabbed it and, just inches ahead of the shark, swam for her life. She and Flounder swam out of the ship and went spiraling up around the mast of another.

Bonk! In his panic Flounder banged into the mast. The blow stunned him, and he sank slowly down toward the ocean floor.

Ariel sped to catch her friend before the shark did. She reached through the ring of an enormous anchor and snatched Flounder just inches from the ground.

With the shark advancing rapidly toward them, Ariel and Flounder popped back through the ring. Flounder had now recovered from his blow, and he and Ariel swam off as quickly as they could.

The speeding shark was concentrating so hard on his prey that he swam straight into the ring, where his neck became stuck tight. He wriggled angrily, but the ring held fast.

Flounder, sensing that the danger had now passed, turned back and stuck out his tongue. "You big bully!" The shark growled with fury, and Flounder recoiled in fear.

Ariel couldn't help chuckling. "Flounder, you really *are* a guppy," she said.

"I am not!" Flounder protested as the two friends made their way up to the surface.

CHAPTER THREE

When Ariel and Flounder burst through the surface of the water, they were greeted by a glorious sunny day. They blinked to adjust to the sunlight, and then Ariel spotted Scuttle lounging on a rock and singing a song out of tune.

The two friends swam quickly toward him, calling out, "Scuttle!"

Scuttle was a plump, jolly gull. He had a big heart, and he loved jokes. Although he wasn't the brightest of birds, he always *sounded* as if he knew what he was talking about.

"Scuttle, look what we found!" Ariel held out her sack.

"Human stuff, huh?" Scuttle said. He reached in and pulled out a fork. "Wow! This is special. This is very, very unusual!"

"What is it?" Ariel asked.

"It's a...a dinglehopper!" Scuttle replied. "Humans use these little babies to straighten their hair out." He demonstrated by combing his head feathers.

"Wow, a dinglehopper," Ariel said with admiration.

"What about *that* one?" Flounder asked as Scuttle took out the tobacco pipe.

"This I haven't seen in years!" Scuttle replied. "It's a banded, bulbous snarfblatt. It dates back to prehysterical times when humans used to sit around and stare at each other all day. It got very boring, so they invented this snarfblatt to make fine music. Allow me." He took a deep breath and blew into the pipe.

Seaweed and water gushed out the top. "It's stuck," Scuttle said with a groan.

Music. The word made Ariel remember the concert. "Oh my gosh!" she cried. "I'm late! My father's going to kill me. I've got to go—but thank you, Scuttle!"

Scuttle gave Ariel back the pipe. "Anytime, sweetie!"

He watched Ariel and Flounder dive beneath the surface and waved until they were out of sight.

Someone else was watching, too—someone not so friendly. In a dark corner of the sea lay the lair of Ursula the Sea Witch. Ursula had two arms and long black tentacles. She was enormous, she was ugly, and she was greedy. Worst of all, she was bent on destroying King Triton.

In a crystal ball that floated above Ursula's cauldron, an image of Ariel and Flounder shone brightly. Ursula stared at it intently. Flotsam and Jetsam, her two eel assistants, hovered nearby. They each had one yellow eye and one white eye that glowed with evil.

"Yes, hurry home, Princess," Ursula said in a mocking tone. "We wouldn't want to miss Daddy's celebration now, would we?"

Now, as always, all Ursula could think about were the good old days, the days when she had lived at the palace—before King Triton had thrown her out of the kingdom.

All Ursula could think about was revenge.

"Look at me!" she cried. "Banished and exiled while Triton and his flimsy fish folk celebrate! Well, I'll give them something to celebrate soon enough. Flotsam! Jetsam! Keep an extra-close watch on this pretty little daughter of his. She may be the key to Triton's undoing!"

CHAPTER FOUR

Ariel stood before her father in the throne room, her head bowed slightly while he scolded her for missing the concert. Flounder hid behind the throne room door.

"I just don't know what we're going to do with you, young lady," the King bellowed, the disappointment in his voice clear. "As a result of your careless behavior, the entire celebration was—"

Suddenly his flowing white beard parted. Sebastian peered out and said, "Ruined! It was ruined! Completely destroyed. This concert was to be the pinnacle of my entire career. Now, thanks to you, I am the laughingstock of the entire kingdom!"

Flounder hated to hear Ariel being yelled at. Before he could even think to stop himself, he swam toward the throne.

"It wasn't her fault!" he cried out, suddenly aware that he now had the full attention of both Sebastian and the King. He was instantly nervous. "Well, um, first this shark chased us, but we got away. Then there was this sea gull, and—"

"*Sea gull?*" King Triton bellowed.

Whoops. Flounder quickly hid behind Ariel.

"You went up to the surface again, didn't you?" King Triton said. "How many times must we go through this? You could have been seen by one of those barbarians, by one of those humans! Do you think I want my youngest daughter to be snared by some fish-eater's hook?"

"But Daddy, I'm sixteen years old," Ariel began in her defense. "I'm not a child anymore!"

"Don't you take that tone of voice with me, young lady," the King thundered. "As long as you live under *my* ocean, you'll observe *my* rules!"

"But if you would only listen—"

"Not another word! And you are *never* to go to the surface again. Is that clear?"

Ariel tried to stare at her father to show him that she wouldn't back down. But it was no use. She could feel her lip start to quiver and her eyes start to tear. She turned and swam out of the throne room, with Flounder following close behind.

King Triton sighed. It was not easy being tough on his daughters; he loved them so dearly.

"Do you think I was too hard on her?" he asked Sebastian.

"Definitely not!" Sebastian replied. "These teenagers, they think they know everything. You give them an inch, they swim all over you! Why, if Ariel were my daughter, I'd show her who was boss. None of this flitting to the surface and other such nonsense. No, sir, I'd keep her under tight control!"

King Triton sat back. Sebastian was giving him an idea. "You know, you're absolutely right, Sebastian," he said. "Ariel needs constant supervision."

"Constant!" Sebastian echoed.

"Someone to watch over her, to keep her out of trouble."

"All the time!"

"And you are just the crab to do it!"

Sebastian froze. That was not what he had in mind. Taking care of Ariel would be a full-time job. He was the royal court composer, not a baby-sitter. But he knew there would be no arguing with the King. When the King asked you to do something, you did it.

Sebastian sank into his shell. Muttering to himself, he swam away from the King's chamber and out into the ocean, where he caught sight of Ariel and Flounder. They were looking around suspiciously—as if they didn't want to be followed.

"Hmm," Sebastian said. "I wonder what that girl is up to now." He swam off behind Ariel and Flounder, hiding in the shadows.

The two friends came to a rock wall in front of which

a large boulder was lodged. With a grunt and some effort, Ariel pushed the boulder aside.

Sebastian gasped. Behind the huge rock was the opening to a dark grotto. Ariel and Flounder disappeared inside.

Thrusting his tiny legs forward as quickly as he could, Sebastian raced in after them. He hid in a corner and looked around in wonder.

The cave was enormous. It rose so high Sebastian couldn't see the ceiling. On the shelflike crags in the walls he could make out small objects: vases, plates, books, clocks, candle holders, eyeglasses, a harp. Sebastian had never seen such things, but he knew they must have come from the human world.

"Oh, Flounder," Ariel said, sitting gloomily on the cave floor. "If only I could make Father understand. I just don't see things the way he does. I don't see how a world that makes such wonderful things could be so bad." She swam upward, admiring all her treasures. "What I wouldn't give to see what the human world is like!"

Sebastian was listening so intently to Ariel that he backed right into a beer stein. With a *thunk*, the top swung shut and the stein fell over and rolled off the edge of a crag. It bumped down the wall and crashed onto the cave floor.

"Sebastian!" Ariel cried in shock.

Sebastian lay in a tangle of knickknacks. "Ariel, what is all this?" he said as he stood up quickly.

"It's just my collection," Ariel replied.

"If your father knew about this place, he'd—"

"You're not going to tell him, are you?" Flounder asked.

"Oh, please, Sebastian," Ariel pleaded. "He would never understand."

Sebastian took Ariel's hand and began pulling her toward the cavern's entrance. "You're under a lot of pressure down here, Princess," he said. "Come with me. I'll take you home and get you something warm to drink."

Ariel felt a shadow pass over them. She looked up at the small opening, way above them, at the top of the cave.

"Hmm, what do you suppose *that* is?" Ariel murmured. She slipped out of Sebastian's grip and swam upward.

"Ariel!" Sebastian screamed, and swam after her. He could hardly believe that after everything that had just happened, the little mermaid was heading for the surface again!

CHAPTER FIVE

Sebastian was furious. He certainly had no business being above the water. And there were Ariel and Flounder, just bobbing in the water, looking at something straight ahead of them.

"Ariel," Sebastian said, demanding an explanation. "What are you—"

KABOOOOM! An explosion cut Sebastian off. He turned around and gasped in shock. A large three-masted ship lay anchored in the water close by. Fireworks from the ship lit up the night sky in bright colors, their sparks floating gently down to the water.

The next thing Sebastian knew, Ariel was swimming toward the ship. She ignored his calls to return at once, as she was so intent on seeing what was happening on board.

Ariel peeked through an opening in the side of the ship, hidden by the darkness. She watched as a shipful of sailors in striped shirts and brown trousers laughed and sang and danced.

What fantastic things their legs were! she thought. The men used them to leap, skip, jump, and dance.

Barbarians? Was that what her father had called humans? They sure didn't look that way to Ariel.

There was a shaggy, furry creature on board that barked and jumped around on four legs. When it saw Ariel, it bounded over and licked her face.

"Max!" called a strong voice. "Here, boy!"

The dog leapt happily over to one of the young men.

The man laughed, and his cheeks dimpled. His dark hair fell across his forehead as he lifted a fife to his mouth.

Ariel had never stared at anyone this way. This man was so different from the rest. Her breath caught in her throat. He was *beautiful*.

Scuttle flapped his way next to Ariel and interrupted her thoughts. "Hey there, sweetie!" he called loudly. "Quite a show, huh?"

"Be quiet, they'll hear you!" Ariel said, grabbing Scuttle's beak. "I've never seen a human this close before. He's very handsome, isn't he?"

Scuttle looked at Max. "He looks kind of hairy and slobbery to me."

"Not that one," Ariel said with a laugh. "The one playing the snarfblatt!"

An older human began shouting, "Silence! Silence!" He stood by a large object covered with a canvas. As the music

fizzled out, the older man announced, "It is now my honor and privilege to present our esteemed Prince Eric with a very special, very expensive, very large birthday present."

"Hurrah!" shouted the men. Some of them clapped the handsome sailor on the back.

Ariel leaned forward to listen.

Prince Eric blushed and said, "Ah, Grimsby, you ol' beanpole, you shouldn't have!"

He's humble, too, Ariel thought. She liked that.

With a smile, Grimsby pulled off the canvas sheet. It fell to the deck, revealing a statue of Eric underneath.

All the sailors applauded. Grimsby looked proud of himself. But Eric thought that while the *face* on the statue looked like his, the pose certainly wasn't him. This figure looked the part of a conquering hero. His chest was puffed

out with pride, he gripped a sword in his hand, and he looked
about to scramble up a rock.

"Gee, Grim, it's...uh, it's really something," Eric managed
to say.

"Well, I had hoped it would be a wedding present, but..."

Eric chuckled. "Come on, Grim, don't start that again."

"Oh, Eric," Grimsby said with a sigh. "It isn't me alone. The
entire kingdom wants to see you happily settled down with the
right girl."

Eric walked to the railing and looked out to sea. Ariel followed him with her eyes, hypnotized. "Oh, she's out there some-
where. Believe me, Grim, when I find her, I'll know. It'll just hit
me, like lightning."

BOOOOOM! As if on cue, a thunderclap sounded, and lightning bathed the ship in harsh light. "Hurricane a-coming!" a sailor shouted. "Stand fast; secure the rigging!"

The crew leapt into action. They quickly tied down the sails and ropes. A huge wave rose over the ship, crashing over Ariel's head. A few yards behind her, Flounder and Sebastian disappeared under the water. Scuttle flapped his wings, but the wind forced him backward. "Ariel!" he shouted.

Ariel tried to hold on to the ship, but it was impossible. She plunged into the sea, head over tail. Struggling against the current, she fought her way upward.

She got back to the surface just in time to see a crack of lightning strike the ship. Instantly the mainsail went up in flames.

Ariel watched in horror as the flames spread. She saw Eric at the steering wheel, trying to guide the ship away from a sharp outcropping of rocks.

CRASH! With a sickening sound, the ship's hull bashed into the rocks. Sailors slid across the deck. Eric lost his balance. He hurtled into Grimsby. Flailing their arms, they both fell overboard.

They landed near a rowboat that the first mate had cut loose from the ship. "Grim, hang on!" Eric shouted. He hopped aboard the rowboat and pulled Grimsby in after him.

"Arf! Arf!"

Above the roaring tempest, Eric heard Max's bark. His eyes darted toward the ship. It was engulfed in fire—and Max was trapped.

Eric dove overboard and swam against the raging sea. Gasping for breath, he finally reached the burning ship and climbed aboard.

"Max!" Eric called, pulling himself up on deck.

CRRRAAACK! Above Eric, the mainmast broke. It tumbled downward, burning like a mammoth torch. Flames immediately began to spread right down to the lower deck, where the room holding the fireworks and gunpowder was.

Eric jumped away and looked up to see Max standing on the top of a staircase. He was shaking, afraid to jump.

"Come on, boy!" Eric held out his arms. "Jump!"

Max barked again and looked about fearfully. Finally, on unsteady legs, he jumped into Eric's arms.

Eric ran with Max to the railing, but his foot broke through the wooden deck and became firmly stuck there. The force of the sudden stop caused Eric to toss Max over-

board. The dog landed in the water with a splash and
swam to the safety of the rowboat.

Before Eric could dislodge his foot, the fire reached the
explosives room. And as Grimsby and the others watched
helplessly from the rowboat—and Ariel looked on in horror
from the water—the ship was blown sky-high in a smoky
ball of flames.

CHAPTER SIX

Ariel felt as if her heart had stopped. Splinters of wood and pieces of twisted metal were raining down around her. She shielded herself, desperately looking for Eric amid the floating wreckage.

Finally she saw a slumped figure dressed in tattered clothing, clinging to a piece of driftwood. It was Eric. She watched as he slipped off the wood and sank slowly under the water. She swam to him as fast as she could, wrapped her arm around him, and lifted his head above the water. While fireworks exploded all around them, Ariel swam with the unconscious man toward the shore. The waves tossed them up and down. Rain whipped their faces. She wanted so much to swim under the sea, but she had heard that humans could drown. So she just gritted her teeth and kept on going until she reached land.

Scuttle joined Ariel, who sat watching the motionless Prince.

"Is he…dead?" Ariel asked.

Scuttle lifted Eric's bare foot and put it to his ear. "I can't make out a heartbeat."

"No, look, he's breathing," Ariel said. She smiled as Eric let out a small sigh. "He's so beautiful."

Ariel could feel something well up inside her. It was more than joy, more than happiness. A gentle love song formed in her heart, and she began to sing it softly.

Sebastian and Flounder arrived in time to see Eric open his eyes. Sebastian's jaw dropped in shock as Eric blinked and looked straight at Ariel. In his daze and in the glare of the sun he couldn't see her very clearly. But he could hear her song.

And then—"*Arf! Arf!*"—Max came bounding over a sand dune. Barking happily, he jumped on Eric and licked his face.

"Eric!" Grimsby shouted from nearby.

Ariel quickly jumped into the water and swam to a nearby rock, just out of Eric's sight. Sebastian and Flounder followed close behind.

"Eric!" Grimsby said, coming over the dune. "My boy, you do enjoy making me worry, don't you?"

Eric shook his head. He was still dizzy, still not quite conscious. "A girl rescued me…," he mumbled. "She…she was singing. She had the most beautiful voice!"

Grimsby hoisted Eric to his feet. "Ah, Eric, I think you've swallowed a bit too much seawater. Come on now, off we go!"

From her perch Ariel watched them walk over the hill.

"We are going to forget this whole thing ever happened!" Sebastian spoke nervously. "The Sea King will never know. *You* won't tell him. *I* won't tell him. And, I will stay in one piece!"

Ariel wasn't listening. Her mind was still on Eric. He was gone now—over the dune, into a world where she was not allowed. A world of air and trees, of sand and grass; a world of humans.

Someday, she vowed to herself, someday I'll find a way to be part of that world.

Deep in the ocean, Ursula the Sea Witch began to laugh. Her eyes were glued to the crystal ball. In it she could see Ariel. And she recognized the look on the girl's face.

"Oh, it's too easy!" she gloated. "The child is in love with a human. And not just any human—a prince! Her daddy will love that!"

She threw her head back and cackled gleefully. She shot a glance at her garden of shriveled, quivering creatures—her collection of souls. Each ugly mass had once been a merperson, a merperson with a desire so strong he or she had struck up a deal with Ursula. The deal was that Ursula would grant a merperson his or her greatest wish, but the deals always ended not only with unfulfilled dreams but with a place in Ursula's collection. Ursula saw to that.

It was so simple, and so many merpeople fell for it. The more souls Ursula had, the better she liked it.

But the whole collection was nothing compared with what she now had in mind. Her face glowed as she grinned at Ariel's image. "King Triton's headstrong, lovesick girl would make a charming addition to my little garden!" she declared with an evil laugh.

CHAPTER SEVEN

Her sisters could tell that Ariel was in love. She had that faraway look in her eyes and day-dreamed more than ever. They all assumed she'd fallen for a merman. Only Sebastian and Flounder knew the whole truth.

Sebastian paced the ocean floor, worried sick. Ariel sat on a rock above him, plucking the petals of a yellow sea flower.

"He loves me, he loves me not…," she said.

"Okay. So far, so good," Sebastian said. "I don't think the King knows…but it will not be easy keeping something like this a secret for long!"

"He loves me! I knew it!" Ariel exclaimed as she pulled off the last petal.

"Ariel, stop talking crazy!" Sebastian said.

"I've got to see him again. Tonight! Scuttle knows where he lives. I'll swim up to his castle. Then Flounder will splash around and get his attention. Then we'll—"

"Ariel! Will you get your head out of the clouds and back in the water where it belongs? Down here is your home! The human world, it's a mess. Life under the sea is better than anything they've got up there! Safe and happy. Everything is beautiful. Humans like to put us in bowls, and when they get hungry—ha! Guess who is cooked for dinner?"

Sebastian went on and on, gesturing and pacing. When he looked up, Ariel was gone.

"Ohhh," he said with frustration, "somebody's got to nail that girl's fins to the floor!"

"Sebastian!" a voice called from behind.

Sebastian turned to see a sea horse racing toward him. "I've got an urgent message from the Sea King!" the sea horse announced. "He wants to see you right away. Something about Ariel!"

Sebastian gulped. The King had found out! Sebastian's career was over, he just knew it. He had failed to take care of Ariel. The King would surely banish him—if he were lucky.

Shaking, Sebastian swam toward the castle.

In the throne room King Triton chuckled to himself. Imagine! His youngest daughter in love—and that rascal Sebastian had kept it a secret. Who could the lucky mer-man be? he wondered.

When Sebastian entered, the King decided to tease him a bit. "Uh, Sebastian, I'm concerned about Ariel. Have you noticed she's been acting peculiar lately?"

"Peculiar?" Sebastian asked with a smile.

"You know," said Triton, "mooning about, daydream-ing, singing to herself?"

"Oh, ooh, well, I—" Sebastian stammered.

King Triton raised an eyebrow. "Sebastian," he said, "I know you've been keeping something from me."

"K-k-keeping something?"

"About Ariel."

"Ariel?" Sebastian's legs were clattering now.

"Being in love?" King Triton picked up his trident and pointed it playfully at Sebastian. "Hmmm?"

Suddenly Sebastian fell to his knees. He grabbed the King's beard and began to whimper. "I tried to stop her, sir! She wouldn't listen! I told her to stay away from humans! They are bad! They are trouble. They—"

44

King Triton sat bolt upright. His eyes glowed with a fiery rage. *"Humans?"* he bellowed. "What about humans?"

His trident began to glow brightly. He lifted Sebastian to eye level.

Sebastian gulped. He had a lot of explaining to do.

"Come on!" Flounder called to Ariel as he led her into the grotto.

"Flounder, why can't you tell me what this is about?" Ariel pleaded.

"You'll see. It's a surprise!"

Ariel stopped short when she saw what was in the center of the grotto. There, tilted to one side, was the statue of Prince Eric.

"Oh, Flounder, you're the best!" Ariel exclaimed. "It looks just like him. It even has his eyes!"

She floated around it. If only it really were him, she thought. "Why, Eric, you want me to run away with you?" she said with a giggle. "This is all so sudden!"

She twirled around with happiness. The room seemed to spin. She saw the shelves, the hole in the ceiling, the entrance, Sebastian, her father—

Her father!

"Daddy!" Ariel cried.

Flounder darted behind a large chest. Sebastian began biting his claw nervously.

King Triton stepped out of the entrance and into the grotto. In the uneven light his face was etched in shadows. "I consider myself a reasonable merman. I set certain rules, and I expect those rules to be obeyed," he said sternly. "Is it true you rescued a human from drowning?"

"Daddy, I had to!" Ariel protested.

"Contact between the human world and the merworld is strictly forbidden. Ariel, you know that. Everyone knows that!"

"He would have died!"

"One less human to worry about!" King Triton scowled angrily.

"You don't even know him," Ariel said heatedly.

"Know him?" Triton roared. "I don't have to know him. They're all the same—spineless savage harpooning fish-eaters! Incapable of any feeling or—"

"Daddy, I love him!"

Ariel gasped and put her hands to her mouth. She couldn't believe she admitted that to her father. But it was true, truer than anything she had ever said in her life.

The words hit King Triton like a fist. His jaw dropped in shock. "No! Have you lost your senses completely? He's a human, you're a mermaid!"

"I don't care!" she replied.

"So help me, Ariel, I am going to get through to you," the King said through clenched teeth. "And if this is the only way, so be it!"

His trident began to glow a bright, angry orange. He

lifted it high and pointed it at the shelves filled with objects from the human world.

WHAM! A beam of orange light shot from the trident and smashed a candelabra.

WHAM! A ceramic globe exploded into bits.

Ariel's face went pale with horror. "Daddy! No!" she screamed.

WHAM! WHAM! WHAM! One by one King Triton destroyed object after object. Ariel swam to her father's side. "Stop it! Stop it!" she pleaded.

But the King's eyes were focused on the statue now. That must be the human Ariel loved, he reasoned. That was the one who could threaten the lives of everyone in his kingdom. He pointed the trident directly at it.

"*Daaaddddy!*" Ariel screamed.

CCRRRRRRAAACCK! The trident's bolt of energy was enormous. The statue exploded into tiny pieces and fell into all the corners of the grotto.

And that was it. The King gave Ariel another stern glance. Then his trident stopped glowing.

Ariel looked over to where the statue had been. There was now only a flat rock with a few jagged pieces of stone. She put her head down and began to cry.

The King's face softened in sadness at his daughter's unhappiness, and he left the grotto with his head bowed. Slowly Flounder and Sebastian came out of their hiding places. They swam toward Ariel.

"Ariel," Sebastian said softly. "I—"

"Just go away," Ariel replied.

Sebastian nodded. He felt awful. He and Flounder gave each other a look. They knew Ariel needed to be alone so, quietly, with sad faces, they swam away.

Ariel didn't see them go. And she didn't see Flotsam and Jetsam approach, either.

"Poor, sweet child," Flotsam said.

"She has a very serious problem," said Jetsam.

"If only there was something we could do for her."

Flotsam and Jetsam stared at Ariel, trying to look concerned.

Ariel glanced up. She had never seen these two eels before. Their words were kind, but she didn't feel comfortable with them.

"Who are you?" she asked.

"Don't be scared," Flotsam said. "We represent someone who can make all your dreams come true."

"You and your prince," Jetsam added.

"Together forever," they chimed at the same time.

"I—I don't understand," Ariel said warily.

Flotsam grinned. "Ursula has great powers."

"The Sea Witch?" Ariel was filled with disgust. "Why, that's...I couldn't possibly. No! Get out of here! Leave me alone!"

"Suit yourself," Jetsam said, turning to swim away.

"It was only a suggestion." As Flotsam left, he swam over the rubble of Prince Eric's statue. The face was lying there, staring blankly upward. Flotsam flicked it with his tail, and it rolled toward Ariel.

Ariel gently picked up the broken sculpture. It was an amazing likeness.

Spineless. Savage. Incapable of feeling. King Triton's words came back to her. How could anyone call Eric those things? Her father was wrong, so wrong!

She looked around. Shattered pieces of her collection lay strewn about. Her beautiful grotto was now a junk pile. And why? Because of her father! Who was really the savage one? Who was the one incapable of feeling?

Ariel's eyes filled with tears. The grotto became blurry. Flotsam and Jetsam were now two distant shadows moving away. In a moment they would be gone.

"Together forever," they had said. But what if it was a trap? What if Ursula had some sinister plan?

Ariel sighed. She couldn't imagine how her life could be any worse than it was now....

"Wait!" The word flew out of Ariel's mouth before she could think. "I'm coming with you."

Flotsam and Jetsam both turned around. As they smiled, their eyes seemed to pulse with electricity. "Wonderful choice, my dear!" Jetsam said.

As the eels led Ariel out of the grotto, they passed by Flounder and Sebastian.

"Ariel!" Sebastian gasped. "Where are you going? What are you doing with this riffraff?"

"I'm going to see Ursula," Ariel retorted.

"Ariel, no!" Sebastian said. "She's a demon!"

Ariel didn't have much use for Sebastian now. After
all, he was the one who had betrayed her. "Why don't you
go tell my father?" she taunted. "You're good at that!"

Ariel turned and swam away. Sebastian and Flounder
hurried after her as quickly as they could.

CHAPTER EIGHT

Ariel hesitated when she reached Ursula's lair. The entrance was the open jaw of an enormous fish skeleton shrouded in puffs of black smoke. The smoke curled around the jaw's pointed fangs.

"This way," Flotsam and Jetsam urged.

Ariel gulped but swam on.

Suddenly something cold and slimy grabbed Ariel's wrist and yanked her downward. She shuddered. It was a shivering, sad-eyed lump, one of many such creatures who moaned and quivered and looked at Ariel with terrified yellow eyes. Gasping with horror, Ariel pulled herself loose.

"Come in, come in, my child," Ursula called.

Ariel spun around. The Sea Witch was leering down at her.

Ariel backed away in fear. This trip didn't seem like such a good idea anymore.

Ursula slid across the seafloor and heaved her massive body toward a vanity table. She admired herself in the mirror and applied lotion to her hair.

"Now then," she began, "you're here because you have a thing for this human, this prince fellow. Not that I blame you. He is quite a catch, isn't he? Well, angelfish, the solution to your problem is simple."

Ursula painted her lips a bright red and gave a twisted smile. "The only way to get what you want is to become a human yourself."

"Can you change me into one?" Ariel asked.

"My dear sweet child, that's what I do. It's what I live for. To help poor, unfortunate merfolk like yourself. Poor souls with no one else to turn to. Many have come to me for my help…and for a price, I grant their wishes." Ursula glanced at the souls huddled by the entrance. "Of course, some can't pay the price, but you needn't worry about that."

Ariel's mouth opened in disbelief. Those horrible-looking creatures were once ordinary merfolk! But because they couldn't pay Ursula's "price," they were lost forever.

"Now here is the deal," Ursula said, pulling Ariel close. As she led Ariel away from the souls, Sebastian and Flounder swam to the entrance. In shock, they stopped and watched.

"I will make you a potion that will turn you into a human for three days," Ursula continued. "You must get dear old Princie to fall in love with you. If he gives you the kiss of true love before the sun sets on the third day, you'll remain human permanently. But if he doesn't, you turn back into a mermaid—and you belong to me!"

"No, Ari—" Sebastian started to scream, but Flotsam quickly wrapped himself around Sebastian's mouth while Jetsam grabbed Flounder.

"Have we got a deal?" Ursula asked before Ariel could notice Sebastian and Flounder.

"If I become human," Ariel said, thinking out loud, "I'll never be with my father or sisters again."

"That's right, but you'll have your man," Ursula replied with a broad smile. "Oh, and there is one more thing. We haven't discussed the subject of payment."

"But I don't have anything!" Ariel said.

"I'm not asking much. Just a token, really. A trifle. You'll never even miss it." Ursula smiled reassuringly. She gave Ariel a gentle touch under the chin. "What I want from you is your voice."

"My...voice?" Ariel couldn't believe her ears.

"That's right; you've got it. No more talking, singing, zip!"

"But without my voice, how can I—"

"You'll have your looks and your pretty face. And you can use body language! Men aren't impressed by conversation. They like women who are demure and quiet."

Ursula proceeded to grab flask after flask of liquid off a shelf and toss them into a cauldron. Ariel watched in fright as pinkish

smoke began to rise. It mushroomed and puffed and swirled around. In the midst of its billows Ariel could see Eric's face form.

"So, have we got a deal?" Ursula asked. She flicked her wrist, and a large golden scroll appeared.

Although Ariel was still very much afraid of Ursula, she leaned forward to read the inscription on the scroll: I Hereby Grant unto Ursula the Witch of the Sea One Voice, for All Eternity. Signed, _____.

In a flash of light, a pen materialized above Ariel's head. "Go ahead," Ursula said. "Make your choice, dear."

Everything was happening so fast. Ariel didn't feel quite right about making a deal with Ursula. But it all did seem rather

simple. So, mustering up all her courage, Ariel grabbed the pen and signed her name.

Ursula's eyes glowed with victory. A horrible, wicked smile came across her face. She waved her arms over the cauldron, chanting a magic spell. The smoke swirled like a tornado, and from the cauldron rose two green, smoky hands.

"Now sing!" Ursula commanded.

Ariel obeyed, and as she sang, a bright light began to glow within her throat.

The long green hands reached toward Ariel and plucked the light from her throat.

Ariel's hands instinctively went to her neck. She was no longer making any sounds, but her *voice* was still singing. Her voice was inside the light!

Ursula began to laugh. She held up a seashell locket that hung around her neck and watched in satisfaction as the hands placed the light inside.

Cackling with glee, Ursula waved her hand over the cauldron again. Enormous blasts of smoke shot upward, and a huge orange bubble encircled Ariel.

Ariel flailed desperately. She flipped her tail, trying to swim away. Then, in two flashes of light, her tail was gone. So was the bubble.

She looked down. Where her tail had been, there were now two legs.

Ariel couldn't breathe. She tried to swim, but she was not used to her legs. She felt strangely weighted down. Was *this* what it was like to be human? Was this…drowning?

Sebastian and Flounder broke loose from Ursula's eels. They grabbed Ariel and raced with her toward the surface.

CHAPTER NINE

Prince Eric sighed. Since his rescue, he hadn't been the same. All he could think about was that girl on the beach.

According to Grimsby, she was just a figment of Eric's imagination.

It was true that Eric hadn't seen her very clearly. He had been too groggy. But there was one thing about her that Eric could never have dreamed up—one thing so beautiful it *had* to be real.

Her voice.

He wanted so badly to hear that girl sing once more. No sound on earth had ever seemed so lovely to him.

Eric picked up his fife and began to play. A sad tune floated across the beach and echoed off the stone wall of his castle.

As the last notes of his song faded away, Eric began walking down the shore. Soon Max was panting along beside him.

Eric tousled the dog's hair and smiled. "Max, I can't get that voice out of my head," he said. "I've looked everywhere for her. Where could she be?"

He paced silently on the sand, hoping against hope he might find her.

Ariel, Sebastian, and Flounder lay exhausted from their swim, on a pile of rocks near where Prince Eric was walking. Ariel slowly lifted her head and blinked in the brightness of the sun. Not too far away, she saw an old shipwreck rotting on the sand. Where was she?

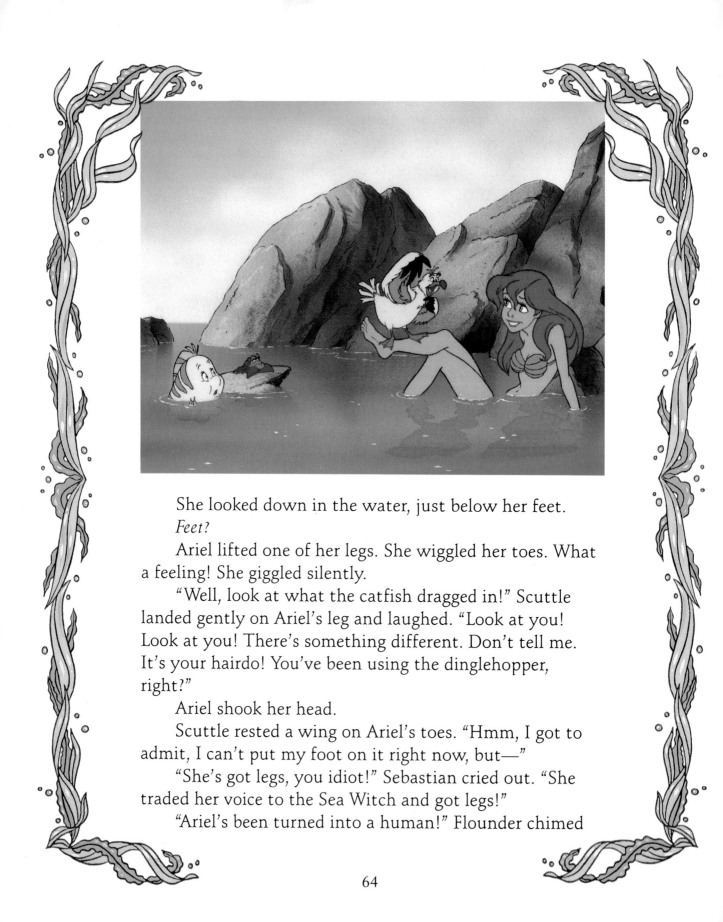

She looked down in the water, just below her feet.
Feet?

Ariel lifted one of her legs. She wiggled her toes. What a feeling! She giggled silently.

"Well, look at what the catfish dragged in!" Scuttle landed gently on Ariel's leg and laughed. "Look at you! Look at you! There's something different. Don't tell me. It's your hairdo! You've been using the dinglehopper, right?"

Ariel shook her head.

Scuttle rested a wing on Ariel's toes. "Hmm, I got to admit, I can't put my foot on it right now, but—"

"She's got legs, you idiot!" Sebastian cried out. "She traded her voice to the Sea Witch and got legs!"

"Ariel's been turned into a human!" Flounder chimed

in. "She has three days to make the Prince fall in love with her, and he's got to kiss her."

Ariel couldn't say a word now, but she still felt wonderful. Carefully she tried to stand on her new legs. Boy, did they feel shaky! She didn't know how humans could possibly—

SPLASH! She toppled over and landed in the water.

"Just look at her!" Sebastian said. "Oh, this is a catastrophe. Her father is going to kill me! I'm going to march myself straight home now and tell him—"

Ariel lifted him up and shook her head, silently begging Sebastian to change his mind.

"Well, maybe there's still time," Sebastian said, trying to convince Ariel that this was the right thing to do. "If we could get that witch to give you back your voice, you could go home with all the normal fish and just be—" The expression on Ariel's face made him stop. He'd never seen her so sad. With a sigh, he finished his sentence. "Just be miserable for the rest of your life. All right, all right, I'll try to help you find that prince."

Ariel gave Sebastian a kiss. As she lowered him to the rock, he muttered, "Boy, what a soft shell I'm turning out to be."

"Now, let's put some clothing on you," Scuttle said, flying toward the nearby shipwreck. "I'm telling you, if you want to be human, the first thing you have to do is dress like one."

Scuttle pulled a white sail and some rope off the shipwreck and brought them to Ariel, who had waded to shore. She draped the sail around her and tied it in place with the rope.

"You look sensational, kid!" Scuttle said.

Ariel looked at Sebastian and Flounder. Before they could react, a loud sound came over a nearby dune.

"Arf! Arf!"

Flounder screamed and dove underwater. Scuttle flew off. Sebastian leapt into a fold of Ariel's costume.

Max came bounding over the dune. He ran to Ariel and began licking her.

"Max! Hey, Max, what's gotten into you, fella?"

It was Eric's voice. Ariel looked toward the dune. And then, in an instant, there he was, looking at Ariel. Max tore himself away and ran toward his master.

"Are you okay, miss?" Eric asked. "I'm sorry if Max scared you. He's really harmless."

Ariel smiled. Eric was so handsome, so gentle. She wished she could say something to him. Instead she blushed and smiled.

"You seem familiar to me," Eric said. "Have we met?"

Max got behind Eric and pushed him closer to Ariel. "We have met!" he said, taking Ariel's hands. "You're the one I've been looking for! What's your name?"

Looking into his eyes, Ariel knew she was in love. Quickly she opened her mouth to say "Ariel," but no sound came out.

"What is it?" Eric asked. "You can't speak?"

Sadly Ariel shook her head.

"Oh, then you can't be who I thought," Eric said, disappointed.

But Ariel was determined not to give up. She began pantomiming what had happened. She pointed to her throat, made swimming motions with her hands, and pretended to pass out. Then she slipped from her rock and fell right into Eric's arms.

"Whoa, careful!" Eric clutched her tightly. "Gee, you must have really been through something. Don't worry, I'll help you. Come on."

Ariel felt unsure on her new legs, but Eric patiently helped her walk. Behind them, Flounder and Scuttle smiled and waved and wished her good luck.

CHAPTER TEN

At the castle Ariel was turned over to Eric's housekeeper, Carlotta. Carlotta drew a hot bubble bath for Ariel and sent her sailcloth dress to the washroom. Then she found a lovely pink ball gown for Ariel to wear to dinner.

Sebastian, however, had a very different experience. Hidden in Ariel's sailcloth dress, he traveled to the washroom, where he was dumped into the wash basin. The soapy water made him cough and sputter. He grabbed on to a shirt in the wash, and when one of the housemaids hung the shirt out to dry, Sebastian went with it.

He lifted his head and peered out the shirt pocket. The clothesline was next to an open window in the castle. Sebastian jumped inside, and with a small thump, he landed on a wooden table. He sighed with relief.

Then he saw the knife—a huge knife stuck in the table between two cut-up halves of a fish. Sebastian looked away in horror—and saw two stuffed crabs on a plate.

Stuffed crabs!

Sebastian gasped in horror. All around him were creatures from the sea—stuffed, fried, baked, and broiled. And every one of them was very, very dead.

"What is this? I have missed one!"

Sebastian spun around to see the chef. His white apron was stained with blood, and he held a sharp cleaver in his hand.

"Eeek!" Sebastian screamed.

"You are alive?" Holding the cleaver high, the chef came after Sebastian.

With a yelp, Sebastian ran as fast as his claws could carry him.

In the royal dining room Eric stood silently by the window. He watched the sun slowly setting over the water. The table was set, but Ariel had not yet arrived.

Sitting at the table, Grimsby filled his pipe with tobacco. "Eric," he said, "nice young ladies just don't swim around rescuing people in the middle of the ocean."

"I'm telling you, she was real," Eric insisted. "I'm going to find that girl—and I'm going to marry her!"

Carlotta's voice drifted into the room from the hallway. "Come on, honey," she said. "Don't be shy."

Eric turned to see Ariel, looking magnificent in a beautiful gown. Eric was speechless.

Ariel smiled shyly as she walked in.

"Eric, isn't she a vision?" Grimsby said, showing Ariel to her place at the table.

"Uh, you look wonderful" was all Eric could say.

"Comfy, my dear?" Grimsby said. "It's not often we have such a lovely dinner guest, eh, Eric?"

Ariel spotted a fork beside her plate. A dinglehopper, she thought. She grabbed it and began combing her hair.

Eric and Grimsby stared silently. Whoops, Ariel said to herself. Maybe it was bad manners to use a dinglehopper at the table. She quickly put it down.

Grimsby lit his pipe and began to smoke. Ariel stared at the snarfblatt and smiled.

"Uh, do you like it?" Grimsby asked, holding the pipe out with admiration.

Ariel took the pipe and blew into it. A cloud of black soot flew into Grimsby's face.

"Pkacchh!" Grimsby cried.

Ariel was horrified. Eric and Carlotta burst into laughter.

"Very amusing," Grimsby muttered as he wiped the soot from his face. "Carlotta, what's for dinner?"

"Oh, you're going to love it! Chef Louis has been fixing stuffed crabs!" Carlotta said as she headed for the kitchen.

Ariel felt sick to her stomach. Imagine eating crabs!

Carlotta returned with three plates, each covered with a sterling silver lid. Ariel tried not to look when Grimsby uncovered his plate, but she couldn't believe her eyes when she saw what was on it.

Sebastian!

It was a good thing Ariel had no voice or she would have screamed. She quickly lifted the lid off her plate and gestured for Sebastian to hide there.

"You know, Eric," Grimsby was saying, "perhaps our young guest would like a tour of the kingdom."

Quickly Sebastian skittered across the table and onto Ariel's plate. She slammed the lid closed.

"Well, what do you say?" Eric asked.

Ariel leaned on the lid and nodded with delight.

"Wonderful!" Grimsby said. "Now, let's eat before this crab wanders off my plate...." His voice trailed off. There was only a pile of bread crumbs where his crab should have been.

Ariel breathed a sigh of relief.

So did Sebastian.

That night, Ariel was shown to a splendid guest room. From there she could hear Eric and Max playing in the courtyard. Smiling, she sank into the soft satin sheets of her bed.

On her dresser Sebastian was still picking bits of lettuce and spices from his shell. "This has got to be, without a doubt, the single most humiliating day of my life!" he said. "I hope you appreciate what I go through for you, young lady. Now then, we've got to make a plan to get that boy to kiss you. Tomorrow you've got to look your best. You've got to bat your eyes and pucker up your lips—"

He turned to look at Ariel, but her eyes were already closed. With a shake of his head, Sebastian said tenderly, "You are hopeless, child, you know that?"

Yawning, he walked to the candle and blew it out. Then he curled up next to Ariel on the bed and drifted into a deep sleep.

CHAPTER ELEVEN

O h, what have I done?" King Triton moaned to himself.

All night long his subjects had been searching for Ariel. Now it was morning, and no one had seen her. They had searched every corner of the seafloor.

None of them suspected the truth. None of them would have thought to look on the land, where Ariel and Prince Eric had just set out for a carriage ride. As they sped over a country bridge, Flounder leapt out of the water below. He spotted Sebastian hiding on the side of the carriage.

"Has he kissed her yet?" Flounder called up.

"Not yet," Sebastian answered.

The tour lasted all day. Ariel fell more in love with Eric every minute. They admired the sights, stopped at a country fair, had a picnic, and danced to an outdoor orchestra. Eric bought her a bouquet of flowers and a beautiful new hat. He even offered her the reins of the carriage. In her enthusiasm Ariel made the horses go so fast that the carriage bounced across a cliff.

That evening, Eric took her on a rowboat across a lagoon. The sunset streaked the clouds with spectacular colors. Sitting in that boat, watching Eric row, Ariel could not imagine a greater happiness.

Nearby, Scuttle sat on a rock and watched. Flounder floated in the water below him. "Nothing is happening! Only one day left, and that boy ain't puckered up once,"

Scuttle said. "This calls for a little vocal romantic stimulation."

Scuttle flew up to the branches of a tree, pushing aside some bluebirds. Clearing his throat, he began to sing: *"BRRAAAWK! CAAAAAW! SKRAAACCKK! EEEEK!"*

Ariel knew who it was right away. She cringed.

"Ow, that's horrible," Eric said. "Somebody should find that poor animal and put it out of its misery."

Hiding at the edge of the rowboat, Sebastian rolled his eyes. "I'm surrounded by amateurs," he said to himself. "If you want something done, you've got to do it yourself!"

He dove into the water and broke off the tip of a long reed. Using it as a baton, he summoned the lagoon animals to attention. "First we've got to create the mood!

"Percussion!" Ducks began tapping a soft drumbeat on turtles' shells.

"Strings!" Grasshoppers rubbed their hind legs together to sound like violins.

"Wind instruments!" Reeds vibrated in the gentle breeze. Together they all played a soft love song.

Sebastian sang in a caressing voice. His words urged Eric to kiss Ariel.

"Do you hear something?" Eric asked.

Ariel could only smile and shrug.

"You know," Eric said, "I feel really bad, not knowing your name. Maybe I could guess. Is it…Mildred?"

Ariel made a face and shook her head.

Eric laughed. "Okay, how about Diana? Rachel?"

As the music continued, Sebastian leapt onto the edge of the boat. He whispered up to Eric, "Her name is Ariel!"

"Ariel?" Eric asked.

Ariel nodded.

"Hmm, that's kind of pretty," Eric said. With a broad smile, he took her hand. "Okay, Ariel."

They floated along, hand in hand, to Sebastian's song. Soon a full moon began to rise over the lagoon. It cast its amber light over the still water. Ariel felt her heart quicken. Eric leaned closer. His smiling face drew nearer. He puckered his lips.

Sebastian grinned. Scuttle wanted to cheer. Flounder flipped his tail with excitement. This was it!

Ariel closed her eyes. She puckered her lips as Eric leaned closer...and closer...and closer...

SPLASHHHHH!

The rowboat flipped over, and Ariel and Eric fell into the water. "Don't worry!" shouted Eric. "I've got you!"

All at once, the music stopped. Ducks flew away; turtles ducked underwater. Sebastian groaned. Scuttle and Flounder stared in shock. The romantic mood was broken. The kiss would have to wait for the next day.

Just beneath the rowboat, two shadowy figures laughed. They clasped their tails together, congratulating each other for tipping the boat.

Then, under cover of darkness, as Ursula watched in her crystal ball, Flotsam and Jetsam began to swim home.

"That was a close one," Ursula said to herself. "Too close. At this rate he'll be kissing her by sunset tomorrow, for sure. It's time to take matters into my own tentacles!" From her shelves she pulled a bubbling potion and a glass ball containing a small, delicate butterfly.

She threw the potion and the ball into her cauldron, creating a loud explosion and a big burst of flames.

"Triton's daughter will be mine!" Ursula gloated. "And then I'll make him wriggle like a worm on a hook!"

Ursula cackled. White smoke encircled her. The seashell necklace around her neck began to glow. Over Ursula's laughter, it sang out loud and clear in Ariel's voice.

Then, slowly, Ursula changed. Her enormous body turned slender. Her tentacles became two legs, and her hideous face was transformed into that of a beautiful dark-haired woman.

With a loud thunderclap, Ursula transported herself instantly to the shore near Prince Eric's castle. She waded out of the ocean, singing. To Eric, who was staring out to sea, deep in thought, she appeared at first as a vision. And then, when the glow from Ursula's necklace was reflected in his eyes, she changed into the girl who had saved his life—the one he had been searching for.

The next morning, Ariel awoke to a shout.

"Ariel!"

Her eyes fluttered open. Sebastian was fast asleep on the pillow beside her. The morning sun was coming in through the window—and so was Scuttle.

"Ariel, I just heard the news." Scuttle landed with a thud on her bed. "Congratulations, kiddo, we did it!"

Sebastian turned around and yawned. "What is this idiot babbling about?"

Scuttle grinned. "As if you two didn't know. The whole town's buzzing about the Prince getting married this afternoon!" He jumped onto the headboard and patted Ariel's cheek. "I just wanted to wish you luck. Catch you later! I wouldn't miss it for anything!"

As Scuttle flew out the window, Ariel and Sebastian gasped. *The Prince was getting married?*

Ariel jumped out of bed. She wanted to scream with joy. She picked up Sebastian and twirled around.

Why hadn't Eric said anything? He must have wanted to surprise her. She was dying to see him, so she put Sebastian down and ran out of her room and down the hall. She practically flew down the staircase; she could barely feel her feet touch the ground.

Then, suddenly, she stopped. The blood rushed from her face. Eric was at the foot of the stairs, arm in arm with a gorgeous dark-haired young woman.

Grimsby stood next to the couple. "Well, now, Eric," he said, "it appears that this mystery maiden of yours does in fact exist. And she is lovely." He took the young woman's hand. "Congratulations, my dear."

"Vanessa and I wish to be married today!" Eric announced. "The wedding ship departs at sunset."

CHAPTER TWELVE

How could he?

Ariel kept asking herself that question over and over. Eric had seemed so open, so honest, so kind. And he had been in love with her. She just *knew* it.

She slumped against a pillar on the royal dock. The entire day had passed, and Eric hadn't looked at her even once. It was as if she'd never existed.

Now, under a glorious sunset, Eric's wedding ship was sailing out to sea. Hundreds of people were aboard, laughing and singing. And Ariel had not even been invited.

She buried her head in her arms and began to weep. Alongside her, Sebastian looked on helplessly. From the water below them, Flounder's little sobs floated upward.

At that same moment, Scuttle swooped down over the ship, humming a wedding tune. It would be so exciting to see Ariel get married. He especially wanted to see the bride kiss the groom.

Through a porthole Scuttle could see Ariel fixing her hair and singing. But wait! That dark-haired girl *sounded* like Ariel, but she sure didn't look or act like her.

Scuttle flew closer, and when the girl looked in the mirror, Ursula's reflection looked back out! He heard her say, "Hah! I'll have that little mermaid soon. And when I do, the entire ocean will be mine!"

"The Sea Witch!" Scuttle said to himself.

There was no time to waste. He immediately flew to the dock. "Ariel!" he cried, flustered and out of breath. "I saw the watch—the witch—the witch was watching the mirror and singing in a stolen voice! Do you hear what I'm saying? *The Prince is marrying the Sea Witch in disguise!*"

"Are you sure?" Sebastian said.

"What are we going to do?" Flounder cried.

Ariel sat up. The Sea Witch. She should have known! Ursula had put Eric under a spell.

The sun hovered just above the horizon. Ariel knew that her time was almost up. This was the third day, and she just had to get to Eric before sunset.

Ariel dove into the water. But she'd forgotten that she didn't know how to swim with legs.

Sebastian ran to a row of barrels by the edge of the dock. With his claw, he cut the string that held them together.

The barrels splashed into the water. "Ariel, grab on to one of them!" he called out. "Flounder, take the rope and pull her to the boat! I've got to get to the Sea King. He must know about this."

"What about me?" Scuttle pleaded.

"Find a way to stop that wedding!"

Instantly Scuttle had an idea. He took to the air, and squawking at the top of his lungs, he called out to all the creatures in the area. Bluebirds, flamingos, ducks, seals, dolphins, starfish, lobsters—all of them perked up and followed Scuttle to the wedding ship.

On board the ship, the wedding march had begun. Ursula and Eric were walking down the center of the boat together. Eric's eyes were glazed, his face blank.

Clutching a bouquet of red flowers, Ursula smiled in triumph. The spell was working. Below her chin, the magic

seashell locket glowed brightly. She stole a glance at the sunset. Yes, she thought. I've done it!

"*Grrrrrr...,*" Max growled angrily as she passed him.

Whump! She kicked him with the back of her foot.

Eric and Ursula stopped in front of the minister. Slowly he began the ceremony. Ursula ground her teeth impatiently. The bottom of the sun was now just touching the horizon.

Finally he came to the vows. "Do you, Eric, take Vanessa to be your lawfully wedded wife for as long as you both shall live?"

Eric stared forward in a trance. "I do," he said.

"And do you, Vanessa—"

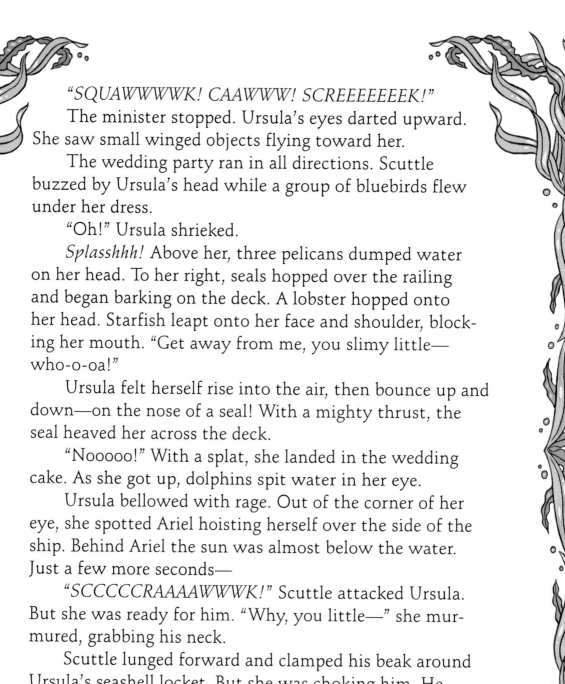

"*SQUAWWWWK! CAAWWW! SCREEEEEEEK!*"

The minister stopped. Ursula's eyes darted upward. She saw small winged objects flying toward her.

The wedding party ran in all directions. Scuttle buzzed by Ursula's head while a group of bluebirds flew under her dress.

"Oh!" Ursula shrieked.

Splasshhh! Above her, three pelicans dumped water on her head. To her right, seals hopped over the railing and began barking on the deck. A lobster hopped onto her head. Starfish leapt onto her face and shoulder, blocking her mouth. "Get away from me, you slimy little— who-o-oa!"

Ursula felt herself rise into the air, then bounce up and down—on the nose of a seal! With a mighty thrust, the seal heaved her across the deck.

"Nooooo!" With a splat, she landed in the wedding cake. As she got up, dolphins spit water in her eye.

Ursula bellowed with rage. Out of the corner of her eye, she spotted Ariel hoisting herself over the side of the ship. Behind Ariel the sun was almost below the water. Just a few more seconds—

"*SCCCCCRAAAAWWWK!*" Scuttle attacked Ursula. But she was ready for him. "Why, you little—" she murmured, grabbing his neck.

Scuttle lunged forward and clamped his beak around Ursula's seashell locket. But she was choking him. He wasn't going to have enough air....

"*Raawwrf!*" Max bolted toward Ursula, mouth open. With a solid clamp, he sank his teeth into Ursula's rear end.

"*Yeeeaaaaaaaaagghhhhhh!*" Ursula shrieked. She let go
of Scuttle. He fell to the deck. The seashell locket hurtled
through the air.

Then, with a small clatter, the shell crashed against
the deck and broke.

Ariel's voice began to sing. In a golden mist her voice
lifted into the air, ringing out over the din, swirling...
swirling...

Right into Ariel's throat.

Ariel stood tall and opened her mouth. It was *her* voice again. She let it grow. She gave it all the sweetness and strength she could.

All other sounds stopped. The birds alighted, and the seals and dolphins slipped happily back into the water.

And Eric snapped out of his trance. He shook his head—and when he looked at Ariel, his eyes were alive again. Alive and filled with amazement. But there was something beyond amazement, too, something that could only be love.

"Ariel?" he said, his voice a hoarse whisper.

Ariel felt like bursting with happiness. She cleared her throat. Then she said her first word as a human—the word she had been wanting to say for three days.

"Eric."

"*Arf! Arf!*" Max jumped beside them, barking happily.

"You can talk!" Eric said. "You *are* the one!"

Ursula looked desperately at the sea. The sun had not quite disappeared. "Eric, get away from her!" she shouted.

But her own voice had returned, harsh and scratchy. She put her hand to her mouth in shock.

"It was you all the time!" Eric said to Ariel, taking her hands.

Ariel drew herself closer to him. "Oh, Eric, I wanted to tell you—" She didn't finish. She didn't need to. Eric was leaning down to her. His lips were a breath away from hers. The setting sun gave its final wink of light on the horizon.

"Eric, no!" Ursula cried.

Eric paused for a split second. The sun slipped below the water.

Ariel suddenly went stiff. Pain shot through her. She pulled away from Eric. "Oh!" she gasped.

"You're too late!" Ursula cried triumphantly. "Haaaah-ha-haaah!"

As Ariel slumped to the deck, she saw Eric staring at her legs. She looked down to see that her tail had returned.

CRRRRACKK! A bolt of lightning lit up the sky and struck Ursula. She surged with power. Her beautiful slinky body began to swell. It burst out of her wedding dress, a giant mass of blubber and tentacles. Ursula was now herself.

All over the ship, wedding guests shouted and fainted. Roaring with laughter, Ursula made her way across the deck. She wrapped her arm around Ariel and sneered at Eric. "So long, loverboy!" she screeched.

Gripping Ariel tightly, she hoisted herself over the railing and jumped.

As Ariel was pulled into the sea, she could hear Eric shouting her name. And through her panic and fear, she could feel her heart breaking.

CHAPTER THIRTEEN

Ursula pulled Ariel downward, toward her underwater lair. Behind them swam Flotsam and Jetsam.

Ariel felt the dark currents rush by her. She longed for the air. She longed for the feeling of legs, the warmth of Eric's glance.

All of that was gone now.

"Poor little Princess!" Ursula gloated. "It's not you I'm after. I've got bigger fish to—"

"URSULA! STOP!"

Ursula pulled up short. In front of her, holding his glowing trident, was King Triton.

Sebastian sat on a nearby rock. He was glad he'd summoned the King in time. "Hmmph," he said, puffing out his chest.

"King Triton, how are you?" Ursula said, grinning.

"Let her go!" King Triton commanded.

Ursula reached forward and gave the King a shove. "Not a chance. She's mine now!" With a blast of magic, Ursula made the scroll appear. "You see, we made a deal!"

Flotsam and Jetsam wrapped their tails around Ariel, holding her prisoner. "Daddy, I'm sorry," Ariel cried. "I didn't mean to! I didn't know!"

King Triton leaned forward and read: I Hereby Grant unto Ursula the Witch of the Sea One Voice, for All Eternity. Signed, Ariel.

With a blast from his trident, King Triton tried to destroy the contract. But the trident had no effect.

"You see," said Ursula, "the contract is legal, binding and completely unbreakable." She shrugged and threw the scroll over her shoulder. It dissolved into a golden swirl and circled around Ariel.

Quickly Ariel began to shrink. She cried out in agony. Her body was shriveling. She was becoming one of the poor souls in Ursula's collection.

King Triton's eyes were wide with horror. But before he could react, Ursula gave him a sly smile. "Of course, I always was a girl with an eye for a bargain. The daughter of the great Sea King is a precious thing to have. But I might be willing to make an exchange—for someone even better!"

Ariel froze. Her father was staring at her. Sorrow lined his face.

The golden swirl lifted from Ariel and hovered in the water. Within it, the scroll materialized again. "Now, do we have a deal?" Ursula asked.

King Triton pointed his trident toward the scroll. It sent out a blast of gold light. Suddenly Ariel's signature disappeared.

Now, at the bottom of the scroll, it said King Triton.

Ursula threw back her head with laughter. "It's done, then!"

Instantly Ariel grew to normal size. The golden swirl began to settle around the King.

"Oh no!" Ariel screamed. "No!"

Slowly King Triton shrank. His crown fell to the ground.

In seconds all that was left of him was a small quivering lump with big, sad eyes.

Sebastian looked at him in shock. "Your Majesty," he whispered sadly.

"Daddy!" Ariel cried out weakly.

Ursula snatched the crown and put it on. "At last it's mine!" She cackled with her newfound power.

Ariel looked up, away from her father. Her own soul now felt hardened. She had disobeyed her father's strictest rule and fallen in love with a human. She had even made a deal with her father's enemy. And after all that, he had still given his soul to save her.

Ariel felt her blood boil. Hate bubbled up within her. "You!" she snarled at Ursula. "You monster!"

Ursula grabbed the trident and pointed it at Ariel. "Don't fool with me, you little brat! Contract or no, I'll blast—"

Shhhhhunk!

A harpoon ripped through one of Ursula's arms. "Yeeeeooooow!" she cried out in pain.

Prince Eric swam above her. "Why, you little fool!" Ursula shouted up at him.

Eric felt as if his lungs were about to burst. He had to go back to his rowboat.

"After him!" Ursula ordered Flotsam and Jetsam.

Eric swam upward and burst through the surface. As he gulped and took in a huge breath of air, Flotsam and Jetsam pulled him back under.

"Come on!" Sebastian shouted to Flounder. They both darted toward Eric. Sebastian pinched Flotsam as hard as he could. Flounder gave Jetsam a whack in the face with his tail.

The eels let go of Eric. But Ursula was prepared. She picked up the trident and aimed it upward. "Say good-bye to your sweetheart!" she said to Ariel.

Ariel grabbed Ursula's hair and pulled. Screaming in pain, Ursula jerked backward. The trident's ray went off

course—and hit Flotsam and Jetsam. With a burst of light, the eels were destroyed.

"My babies!" Ursula cried. "My poor little poopsies!"

Ursula's sadness quickly turned to anger—glowing, steaming anger. Black smoke circled around her.

Ariel swam to the surface. "Eric," she yelled, "you've got to get away from here!"

"No, I won't leave you!" Eric replied.

The sea began to rumble. Eric and Ariel looked down. A gold object rose out of the water and came between them. Ariel felt something solid beneath her, and she and Eric were pushed upward.

Then, like an ancient volcano coming to life, Ursula—a thousand times her normal size—burst through the surface. Ariel and Eric were two mere specks clinging to her crown. Ursula's body cast a shadow that seemed to swallow the sea for miles around.

Ariel and Eric grabbed hands and jumped. "You pitiful fools!" cried the Sea Witch, her voice resounding like a bass drum. Her trident had grown with her, and she swung it high. "Now I am the ruler of all the ocean! The sea and all its spoils must bow to my power!"

The sky cracked with lightning. A wave rose between Eric and Ariel, forcing them apart. "Eric!" Ariel screamed.

Ursula's face was grotesque. Her deep, terrifying laughter boomed out as she swirled the trident in the water.

Eric was drawn into a whirlpool that twisted him violently around. The whirlpool was so powerful, it stirred up the wreckage of an ancient ship from the ocean floor.

Ariel clung to a rock at the bottom of the whirlpool. Above her, in the rapid rush of water, Eric swam toward the shipwreck, grabbed hold, and pulled himself aboard.

The ship's broken mast was jagged and sharp, but its steering wheel was intact. Eric closed his hands around it.

The Sea Witch loomed over the circling waters. She looked down at Ariel and—*CRACK!*—sent a ray toward her, shattering the rock. Ariel jumped away. She landed on the seafloor, in the dead center of the whirlpool.

"So much for true love!" Ursula thundered. Carefully she pointed her trident at Eric's ship.

Eric gritted his teeth. Ursula's face filled the sky. He swung the steering wheel sharply toward her.

The ship lurched, its mast swung wide—and pierced into Ursula's belly.

"*RRRRRRRRAAAWWWWWRRGHH!*"

Ursula's cry of pain blotted out the sound of thunder. Giant lightning bolts tore through the sky. As they struck Ursula, she glowed and sizzled. Screaming, she began to sink. Her tentacles lashed out. One of them swiped against Eric's ship and pulled the ship and Eric underwater.

Then, slowly, like a sinking island, Ursula disappeared forever.

CHAPTER FOURTEEN

s King Triton's trident sank slowly to the ocean floor, the nest of souls was transformed back into merpeople. The sea was filled with their shouts of surprise and delight.

King Triton, too, was restored to his former self. He looked up to see his trident float into view. He grabbed it and smiled.

But there was no time to rejoice. He had to find Ariel. With a powerful thrust, he shot toward the surface.

There he spotted Sebastian and Flounder, who led him to a nearby shore where Ariel was sitting on a rock, staring sadly downward.

At the edge of the sand, Prince Eric lay unconscious.

"She really does love him, doesn't she, Sebastian?" King Triton said.

"Mmm," Sebastian agreed. "Well, it's like I always say: Children have got to be free to lead their own lives!"

King Triton raised an eyebrow. "*You* always say that?"

Sebastian gave the King a nervous glance. Then the two of them broke into laughter. "Well, then, I guess there's only one problem left," the King said.

"What's that, Your Majesty?" Sebastian asked.

King Triton sighed. "How much I'm going to miss her."

Sebastian's jaw fell open in surprise. King Triton raised his trident and sent a beam of light toward Ariel.

Ariel looked up. At the sight of her father, she was filled with happiness. And then her tail was transformed

99

into two legs, and suddenly she was wearing a gorgeous blue dress.

Ariel was human again—this time for good.

Eric began to stir. He sat up, held his head, and looked around. Then he saw Ariel coming toward him out of the ocean.

A smile lit up Eric's face. He ran to Ariel and swept her up in an embrace.

They were free. They belonged to each other.

And finally, they shared a long, long kiss.

To this day, the merpeople still talk of Ariel and Eric's wedding. They tell of the glorious cake and the grandness of the wedding ship. And no one will ever forget King Triton's wedding present.

After Ariel and her father shared a tight embrace, King Triton waved his trident in a great arc, and a dazzling rainbow appeared in the sky. It expressed Triton's hope that the young couple would have a brilliant, colorful future. And they did.

DISNEY'S THE LITTLE MERMAID

Tales from Under the Sea

Illustrated by Fred Marvin

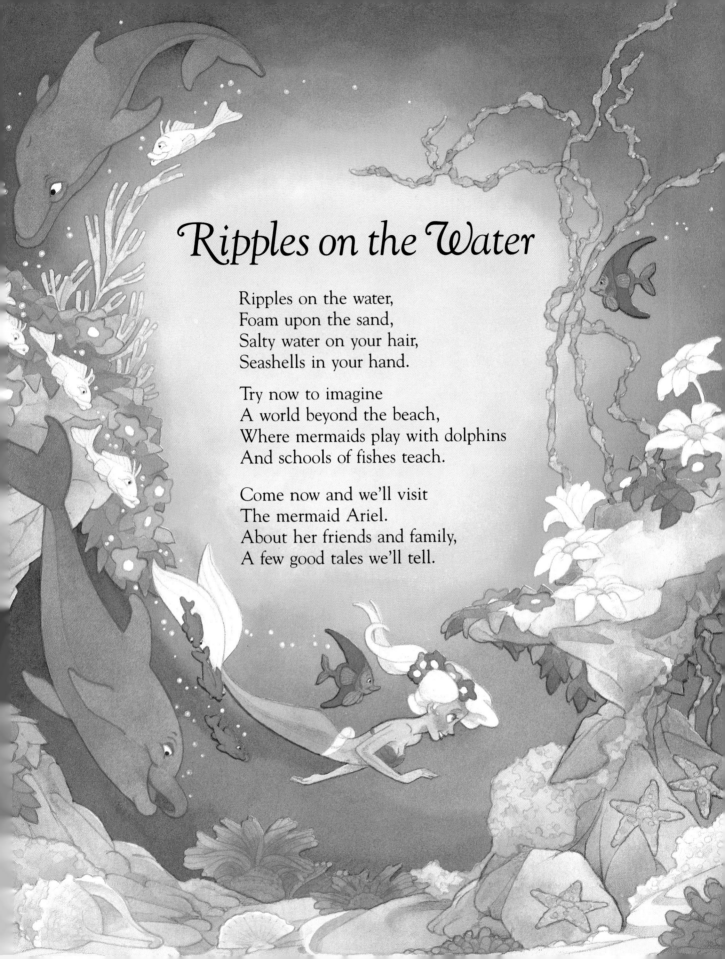

Ripples on the Water

Ripples on the water,
Foam upon the sand,
Salty water on your hair,
Seashells in your hand.

Try now to imagine
A world beyond the beach,
Where mermaids play with dolphins
And schools of fishes teach.

Come now and we'll visit
The mermaid Ariel.
About her friends and family,
A few good tales we'll tell.

THE LITTLE MERMAID
FOLLOWS HER HEART

Beneath the sea, in the Sea King's royal concert hall, there was an important little crab who was anything but happy. Sebastian, the royal composer and conductor, had six of His Majesty's singing mermaid daughters on stage. There should have been seven. Adella, Alana, Andrina, Aquata, Arista, and Attina were all practicing their voice lessons. But Ariel, the youngest of King Triton's daughters, was late—again.

"Ah!" Sebastian called out as Ariel rushed in. "You're here at last! We began half an hour ago, young lady."

"Do-re-mi-fa-so-la-ti-do," sang Adella and Alana.

"Where-were-you-Daddy-wants-to-know?" Andrina and Aquata sang as a scale.

"Daddy was here?" Ariel said nervously.

"Yes," answered Sebastian. "And since he asked me, I could not hide from him the fact that his youngest daughter was late, and is *always* late for her singing lessons."

Ariel gasped. "You told him about all the other times?"

Sebastian rolled his eyes. "My dear, sweet, little mermaid, I am a loyal servant and trusted friend of the King. I cannot lie to your father—he's the boss. He was here, and you were not. And quite frankly, I do not know why you cannot be less tardy; more respectful . . ."

Poor Ariel looked as if she were about to cry.

"Oh, Sebastian," interrupted Arista, "do you have to be so crabby?"

Arista giggled, and soon, all the sisters, even Ariel, were giggling out of control.

"Girls! Young ladies! Princesses! Oh, why does this have to happen to me?" Sebastian wailed.

"Ahem!" A loud voice came from the back of the hall. Sebastian whirled around.

"Your Majesty!" Sebastian cried, and he bowed low.

"Ariel," said King Triton, "it has come to my attention that you have been giving Sebastian here a hard time about these music lessons. This cannot continue.

"I know," said the Sea King more kindly, "that this must be a difficult time for you; you are growing up so fast. But soon you will be sixteen. You can no longer just play the day away."

"I know how important music is," said Ariel, "but sometimes I find myself wondering about..."

"About what, my child?" said Triton, gently.

"Well," said Ariel hesitantly, "ever since I was a very little mermaid I've guessed there is a place above the water where girls sing their songs. I have always wondered what it would feel like to be one of them."

King Triton could hardly control himself. "You are *not* like them, Ariel! They're *humans*! Fish-eating, barbaric *humans*! Ariel, tell me, does your being late have anything to do with this nonsense?"

Like Sebastian, Ariel could not bring herself to lie to the Sea King, so she just hung her head.

"Ariel, whatever you may have heard about humans and their world is nothing more than so many fairy tales. They are very dangerous to us."

"But Daddy, I know in my heart that all humans cannot be bad. When I swim up to the surface and see the clear blue sky and the fluffy white clouds..."

King Triton exploded. "The *surface!* You go up to the *surface?*" The Sea King was so enraged he could no longer trust himself to speak. "Ariel, we will talk about this later," he said, and quickly left the concert hall.

There were tears in Ariel's eyes as she watched him go. She could not

possibly rehearse now. She, too, swam out of the concert hall as quickly as she could. She went straight to a familiar spot, marked by a huge boulder. Her best friend, Flounder, was waiting for her there.

"Let's go inside," said Ariel.

She pushed aside the boulder just far enough to allow them to slide through the opening. On the other side of the big rock was a sunlit cavern full of objects that Ariel had collected from sunken ships lying on the bottom of the sea. Everything that humans made or used was important to Ariel.

"My father is angry at me," said Ariel. "He doesn't like me going to the surface, and he doesn't trust humans at all. He would be even more angry if he knew about all this," she said, pointing to her collection. "But I have such a strong feeling he's wrong about humans, and someday, Flounder, I know I'm going to prove it!"

King Triton

I'm the King of all the waters
With not one, but seven daughters,
So forgive me for a moment if I boast.

But these maids are so delightful,
Never mean, nor rude, nor spiteful,
That I cannot say which one I love the most.

Yes, they're all so very clever,
They say I'm the greatest ever,
And the fish all stop to listen when they sing.

I would give up all I own—
Toss down the crown, get off my throne,
For I know that in their eyes I'd still be King.

ALANA'S GARDENS

Alana was the quietest of the mermaid princesses. She loved to watch beautiful sea flowers grow. She took care of all the gardens around the sea palace and made everything so beautiful that King Triton often brought guests over just to admire her work.

But Alana did not let praise go to her head. It was reward enough to spend her time tending her gardens and looking after all the little sea creatures. She fed minnows from her hands and freed fish caught in fishermen's nets. A turtle she had once rescued refused to leave her side and became her pet.

One day as Alana was pulling weeds in one of the gardens, Arista rode up on a giant seahorse.

"Get up quickly!" she cried. "We have to hide! Ursula the Sea Witch has created a terrible tidal wave, and it's rolling this way!"

Then Arista pulled Alana onto the back of the seahorse, and off they rode to the mountains at the edge of their father's kingdom. In these undersea mountains there were tunnels and caves where the merpeople could hide in times of danger.

Alana and Arista found the rest of the royal family and many other merpeople already there. Within seconds the tidal wave hit. The mountains shook as powerful waves of water poured into the caves, knocking everyone into each other. Alana closed her eyes as rocks and seaweed flew past. Spirals of foam and bubbles were everywhere. The tidal wave roared on and on, and above all the noise the merpeople could hear the evil sound of Ursula's laughter.

When at last it was all over, the shaken mermen and mermaids slowly left the caves to see what was left of the kingdom. Alana swam as fast as she could to the palace. The castle was still standing, but Alana's lovely gardens were ruined! Trees were uprooted—leaving great holes in the ground—shells were smashed, and every single flower had been ripped away.

Just then Alana felt something nudging her elbow. She looked down, and there was her faithful turtle, holding one little sea flower in his mouth.

"Oh!" she sobbed, throwing her arms around his neck. Then she sat up and wiped her eyes. "At least I still have my home—and you," she said, patting her turtle's head.

All that day, and well into the night, everyone in the kingdom worked to restore the land. There was so much to be done. Rocks had to be moved, fallen seaweed cleared away, and sand swept into neat piles. Alana forgot all about her gardens as she and the rest of the merpeople slowly cleaned up.

Finally King Triton came over to Alana and took a heavy shell out of her hands. "Get some rest, daughter," he said, and gave her a kiss. Alana was

too tired to argue, too tired to even return to the palace. She soon fell asleep beside a little patch of coral.

When Alana woke up the next morning she shook her head and rubbed her eyes, unable to believe she wasn't dreaming. All around her flowers bloomed, trees swayed, and shells circled neat little flower beds. Her gardens were back, even more beautiful than before!

Alana saw hundreds of fish, crabs, turtles, and dolphins hovering around her. "Did you . . . ?" she began, still amazed by what she saw.

Yes, they all nodded. Alana's sea friends had spent the night gathering plants, flowers, and trees from the farthest parts of the ocean to thank Alana for all the love and care she had always given to them and to their world.

ARISTA'S WILD RIDE

"There you go," said Arista, patting her giant seahorse's neck. She fed him from her hand, and he whinnied softly for more. "No, Foamy, that's enough," she said. "You don't want to get fat and slow, do you?"

"Those seahorses sure do love you, Princess," said Mackey, the old merman who worked in the royal stables. "You've got a way with them."

"Seahorses are wonderful, Mackey," Arista said, taking off Foamy's bridle. "Sometimes I think they're almost as smart as mermaids!"

Just then Arista and Mackey heard a whinny off in the distance. They swished out of the stables just in time to see a proud-looking golden seahorse speed by them.

"Oh, isn't he beautiful?" Arista whispered, not taking her eyes off him.

"That he is," Mackey agreed. "But a wild one like that would be harder to tame than a tidal wave. I know what you're thinking, Princess, and you can just forget it. No one could ever tame a stallion like him."

But Arista wasn't listening. She was imagining herself riding that magnificent seahorse!

After that, Arista thought about the wild stallion every day. She would see him swimming proudly off in the distance and knew that one day she had to catch and tame him. "One ride," she thought as she groomed the royal seahorses. "One ride and I'll know if I can tame him. But how?" she wondered. "How?"

Then one day Arista thought of a plan. With a large basket over one arm, she began to pick the softest, greenest seaweed she could find. When

she had filled up the basket, Arista carefully set it down under a small cliff where she had often seen the golden seahorse stop for a quick moment before he swam off again.

"Now I'll just wait," Arista said, and she hid, out of sight, on the cliff.

It wasn't long before the water began to ripple and Arista heard the familiar whinny of the wild stallion. He stopped when he spotted the basket of seaweed and then approached it cautiously. Soon he was nibbling on the tender seagrass.

"Now!" Arista told herself, and she darted over the edge of the cliff. She wrapped her arms tightly around the seahorse's neck.

The seahorse was startled. It jerked its head back and whinnied in alarm. But Arista held on and they were off!

Arista had never been so excited. The seahorse raced through the ocean, going faster and faster. Arista saw the blur of surprised mermen and mermaids watching her speed past. She even saw her father, but the seahorse was going so fast she couldn't even call out.

Arista tried to slow the wild stallion down. She tried to pet his neck, to murmur softly to him—all the things her own seahorses loved. But nothing slowed this wild one down. And now Arista was starting to worry. Getting off Foamy and the tame seahorses was easy. You just floated off and swam away. But Arista knew this seahorse was going so fast that she would probably lose her balance and go tumbling head over fins if she got off now. She was afraid of knocking into sharp coral or craggy rocks.

I thought getting *on* was going to be the hard part of this ride! Arista thought to herself as the horse seemed to go even faster and she clutched his neck even tighter.

"Whoa!" Arista cried. But the seahorse did not slow down a bit. Arista and her stallion dashed by an astonished Sebastian. He saw her frightened expression.

"Princess," he called after her, "let go!"

"I'm afraid!" yelled Arista as the stallion picked up speed.

"Hang on then," Sebastian called after her. "Old Sebastian will save you!" And he swam to the stables and mounted Foamy.

"Swim, Foamy, swim!" And they were off. Soon they saw Arista heading back in their direction and going no slower.

"Princess," Sebastian called, "can you let go now?"

"I can't," cried Arista.

"Nothing will happen to you if you do. Of this I assure you. Foamy will swim below you and catch you when you go. But, if you prefer, I will take your hand."

"Oh, yes, Sebastian. Please!" And, with most of the kingdom looking on, Sebastian reached down.

Arista stretched out her arm, but instead of being pulled up by Sebastian, she pulled him down!

"Oh, no, now we're both stuck." Arista shouted to Sebastian, who grabbed on to a lock of the wild seahorse's mane.

"Princess, this is very fast indeed!" Sebastian, too, was afraid to let go.

The golden seahorse turned around and swam toward Foamy, who was now below them.

"It is time now, Princess. We shall both let go at once. I will count to three and Foamy will fetch you up at once on his back. One…two…three."

Arista closed her eyes, clenched her teeth, and—let go! And land she did, right on Foamy. But where was Sebastian? Still locked on tight to the mane with his claws. With the eyes of the kingdom on him, Sebastian knew he had to let go. The little crab tumbled over and over and landed in Arista's basket of seaweed.

Nothing much but Sebastian's pride was wounded. As his friends applauded, he brushed some seaweed off and took a bow.

Arista rode up on Foamy. The golden seahorse had disappeared off into the distance.

"Sebastian, are you all right?" she asked.

"But of course, Princess. Just do me a most large favor and do not try such activities again," replied the crab, trying to rid himself of the last of the seaweed.

"But, Sebastian, don't you think a few more rides like that would tame him?" Arista's cheeks were rosy and her eyes were glowing.

"Princess, just one ride like that was enough to tame *me*! The only fast things I am interested in now are the musical pieces I will conduct! I am going to the concert hall for some peace and quiet!"

And Sebastian scurried off, leaving Arista to dream of her next encounter with the wild seahorse.

ARIEL'S NEW FRIENDS

One morning Ariel went off by herself for a nice, refreshing swim. She had just stopped to rest for a moment when she heard a noise behind her.

"Help! Help!"

"Who's there?" Ariel asked, looking around.

"Help! Over here!"

Ariel turned and saw a young merman. His arm was caught in a giant oyster shell.

"I'm so glad to see you," said the merman. "I've been trapped here for hours!"

"How did you get stuck like this?" asked Ariel. "Were you trying to steal a pearl?"

"No, I wasn't," said the merman. "I'm here because of grouchy Old Driftwood. He lives in that cave over there with his two stingrays, Smudge and Sludge. My older brother dared me to go knock on his door and get him to come out."

"You didn't!" said Ariel.

"I can never refuse a dare, so I went right up and banged on his door."

"Then what happened?" asked Ariel.

"He came out, took one look at me, and grabbed my arm. My brother took one look at Old Driftwood and was off like a shot. The old guy brought me over to this slimy oyster, pried open the shell, stuck my arm in, and left me. I've been here ever since."

"Well," said Ariel, "I'm not strong enough to open the shell, but I think I know another way."

Ariel began to sing, hoping the oyster in the shell would listen and be moved by her request. Her voice was as pure and as brilliant as a single strand of gold.

Open up, open up, beautiful shell
And set this merman free.
Of this act I'll never tell,
And forgiven you shall be.

Slowly, slowly, as Ariel repeated her song the shell began to open. The young merman pulled out his arm and sighed with relief.

"Thanks!" he said with a grin. "You're pretty amazing. What's your name? My name's Gil."

"Hello, Gil, I'm Ariel," said Ariel shyly.

"Not *Princess* Ariel, youngest daughter of King Triton!" said Gil.

"That's me," she said.

Just then, Old Driftwood opened his door slightly and stuck his head out. Eyes blazing, he shook his fist and shouted, "That's it! I've had enough of that racket! Get out of here before I make chowder out of the both of you! Get them, Sludge! Sting them, Smudge!"

The two stingrays burst out from behind Old Driftwood and swam right toward Ariel and Gil.

"Let's go!" shouted Gil, taking Ariel by the hand. They swam as fast as they could, with Sludge and Smudge in hot pursuit. Ariel and Gil swam and swam until they were out of breath, finally losing Sludge and Smudge in a forest of sea kelp.

"Well, you did even better than your brother asked. Not only did you knock on his door, but you even got Old Driftwood to talk to you!" said Ariel.

"Then why do I feel so bad about the whole thing?" asked Gil.

"Could it be because you and your brother were trying to play a trick on a lonely old man?" said Ariel gently.

Gil hung his head. "Do you really think he's lonely?"

"How couldn't he be?" said Ariel. "After all, he lives all the way out there by himself, with no one but two stingrays for company."

"Well, he's still a grouch!" said Gil.

"Did you and your brother ever think that he's grouchy because no one is ever nice to him?"

"Oh," said Gil. "You really *are* amazing. Well, what can we do about it if it's true?"

Ariel thought for a moment. "Come on," she said, taking Gil by the arm.

"Where are we going?" he asked.

"Back to knock on Old Driftwood's door again," answered Ariel. He watched as she began gathering up seagrass, coral, moss, and sparkling shells. She arranged them in a beautiful bouquet.

Gil wrinkled his nose. "That stuff is for girls," he said. "Old Driftwood's not going to like it."

"We'll never know if we don't try," said Ariel.

When they arrived at Old Driftwood's cave, Ariel went right up to the door and softly knocked once. She dropped the bouquet on the doorstep and swam off. A few minutes passed before Old Driftwood opened his door. Sludge and Smudge glided out in front of him.

"What's this?" he said. "A bouquet, eh?" He looked around and saw Ariel and Gil.

"What do you young merpeople want with me, anyway?" he called out.

"We would just like to visit with you awhile, sir," said Ariel as politely as she could.

"That's right," said Gil. "Could you, uh, could you tell us about when you were young?"

That seemed to be just the right thing to say. Old Driftwood's eyes lit up.

"When I was young? Do you really want to know about that?"

"Yes, please!" said Ariel and Gil.

"Well, come on in. Sludge and Smudge won't hurt you," said Old Driftwood with a smile. "They're all zing and no sting.

"Why, when I was young we liked to play tricks on the sailors. We'd knock on the bottoms of their fishing boats and get them wondering what was going on right beneath them! Ha! I've got dozens of stories. Come in, come in!" Old Driftwood ushered the young merpeople into his house.

Much later that afternoon, Gil and Ariel were on their way back home, full of fine seacakes and wonderful stories.

"I'm very glad my brother dared me to knock on his door," said Gil.

"Me, too," said Ariel. "You might ask him to come with us when we go back to visit next week."

And that's just what Gil did.

The Song of Scuttle

A feathery, fluttery
Mess of a bird,
Whose clumsy big feet
Make him look quite absurd.
Is that how you think
Of the seagull Scuttle?
Well, there's more to him
Than just a big muddle!

Now, did you know that
Old Scuttle the Gull
Knows every ship
From its sails to its hull,
That his life has been filled
With adventures and glory?
Well, sit ye, me lads,
And I'll sing you his story.

Scuttle's a friend
To every seafaring man.
He helps us
In every way that he can.
He warns us
Whenever the winds are brewin',
For he knows that a storm
Can be our undoing.

So now to our hero,
Old Scuttle – a toast!
From the men he has saved
As they sailed coast to coast.
Mariners all now attest to his glory,
The mascot of every sloop, raft, and dory!

KING TRITON'S
SPECIAL GIFT

It was King Triton's birthday, and everyone under the sea was preparing for the big celebration that night. The princesses were wrapping presents and decorating the palace, the royal chef was baking a special cake, and Sebastian was rehearsing the Crustacean Band. He had composed a new song in honor of His Majesty, but Minnow just couldn't keep time with the others. The band was getting tired.

"I give up!" Minnow finally said, folding his fins stubbornly. "I'm just too young to be a good musician."

"So you think that if you're young you can't do things, do you, Minnow?" Sebastian asked. "Where would all of us be today if King Triton had felt that way?"

"What do you mean, Sebastian?" Minnow asked.

"Don't you know?" Sebastian asked in surprise. He looked around. "Don't any of you know the story of King Triton and the Sea Witch?"

Everyone in the band shook his head.

"Well, then it's time you heard," Sebastian said.

"Many years ago, Ursula the Sea Witch ruled the kingdom. She lived in the palace and forced all the mermen and mermaids to be her slaves. Oh, she was cruel, that one. She thought she knew more about the ocean than anyone. Well, she was wrong.

"Now, Triton was a very young man when Ursula ruled, but even so, he was determined to free all the merpeople. Everyone told him there was nothing he could do. He was not even a full-grown merman, and Ursula was the most powerful witch of all. But Triton was determined and he had an idea.

130

"Triton began to tell everyone that he had found a pirate's treasure chest buried at the bottom of the sea. He claimed it was filled with diamonds and emeralds and rubies and gold—more riches than anyone could imagine. One day Ursula, too, heard this young merman boast that his treasure was worth far more than all of the riches in the royal castle combined.

"This was more than Ursula could stand. She sent for Triton and demanded to know where this wonderful treasure was. He didn't want to tell her, but when Ursula threatened to imprison him, Triton agreed to take her to it. They swam far away to a gloomy, dark cave. Deep inside there was a treasure chest, half-covered with sand.

"'I'm going to stand back now,' Triton said, and he moved toward the mouth of the cave. 'The bright light flashing from the jewels hurts my eyes.'

"Ursula did not even pay any attention to him. She quickly threw open the lid to the chest. But there was no treasure inside, only the evil Undertow, which pulled her into the chest and down, down, down to the deepest, blackest depths of the ocean. It would take her many, many years to swim her way back.

"Triton quickly returned to the kingdom. When the mermen and mermaids heard what he had done, they all declared him king. And that is how King Triton came to rule the seas."

The fishes were silent for a moment. Then Minnow spoke. "If a young merman is smart enough to conquer the Sea Witch," he said, "I guess a young fish like me can keep time in an orchestra."

The band began to practice again, with a new energy. That night, when the Crustacean Band played their new piece, the King was so pleased he congratulated each member of the band personally. Minnow had never been so proud as when he bowed before the greatest merman in the kingdom.

ANDRINA'S PERFORMANCE

Andrina was the most athletic of all of King Triton's daughters. She won all the trophies for underwater sports, loved playing catch with the mermen, and was always practicing aerobics around the palace. In fact, she was very often swimming or tumbling when she should have been studying literature or history or music. Andrina could simply not sit still long enough to enjoy her studies.

This was a problem for Sebastian. Music and singing were an important part of a royal mermaid's education, and he often had to chase after Princess Andrina to get her to practice her singing. But Andrina's voice was as lovely as those of her sisters. Her singing was so pure and clear Sebastian felt it was well worth the chase.

One morning, as all seven mermaid sisters were practicing their scales, Sebastian had an announcement to make.

"As King Triton's entrusted, humble servant," he began regally, "it is my great privilege to compose a special tribute to His Royal Highness. And I have decided that each of you princesses will sing a piece of your own composition to honor your father."

"Oh, Sebastian!" Ariel cried, clapping her hands. "What a wonderful idea!"

"Can I sing first?" begged Adella.

"I'll pick some flowers for all of us to wear in our hair for the concert," said Alana dreamily.

Aquata, Arista, and Attina began trying out verses at once.

Only Andrina was silent. Compose a piece of music? Add words? She

felt she could never do that. She could barely sit still to sing the words Sebastian handed to her.

"I can't do it," she said.

"Oh, Andrina," said Ariel. "What's the matter? Don't you want to sing for Daddy?"

"Of course I do," Andrina said. "But I can't write my own piece. I'm no good at that sort of thing."

"But you have to!" Adella cried. "It won't be right if everybody sings except you!"

Andrina didn't know what to say, so she swam off by herself.

During the next few days, the whole palace rang with the happy voices of the little mermaids as they tried out the songs they had written. Sebastian had never seen the princesses work so hard.

Only Andrina had yet to write something. She couldn't concentrate. Every time she sat down, she had to get up. What if she did write something and it wasn't any good? What if everyone laughed at her? It was too terrible to think about.

Sebastian was getting worried. The concert was quickly approaching, and he knew King Triton would be very disappointed if Andrina did not perform her own piece. He decided it was time to have a talk with her.

"Andrina, I just don't understand you," he began. "You haven't even written a line. Aren't you trying?"

"But Sebastian, I do try. I'm just no good at this sort of thing," said Andrina.

"Well, if you keep jumping up and rushing off you'll never write anything. Don't you realize, Princess," said Sebastian, "that as long as the piece is from you, your father cannot help but like it?"

But say what he might, Sebastian could not get Andrina to write a single note of music.

The night of the concert arrived and six mermaid sisters eagerly swam to the concert hall, ready to perform their original works. Andrina stayed behind.

"I don't know why it's so easy for Ariel and the others to write music for Daddy," she said, sighing. "Well, it would be another story if they had to race seahorses for him, or swim in competition, or…" A smile began to spread across Andrina's face. She knew just what to do as a tribute for her father.

Andrina swam quickly to the concert hall and whispered a few words to Sebastian before taking her seat. Her sisters were delighted but very puzzled. What would Andrina do? When her turn came, Sebastian signaled the band to play the Sea King's favorite song, and while Andrina sang it, she gave the audience the best acrobatics show they had ever seen! And King Triton loved every minute of it, too, since he knew Andrina's act came straight from the mermaid's heart.

Under the Ocean

Under the ocean,
There was quite a commotion,
When two mermaids went out to play.

A seashell they spied,
"It's mine!" they each cried,
As each shoved the other away.

They started to fight.
Soon the seashell got buried
Away out of sight.

A lesson was learned,
And so homeward they turned,
Ashamed of what they had done.

For it's better to share
When there's only one there,
And selfishness spoils the fun.

ADELLA AND
THE PINK PEARL

Princess Adella loved to look at herself in the mirror. She believed she was the ocean's most beautiful mermaid and would tell that to anyone who cared to listen. Her sisters did not care to listen. Adella told them anyway.

One evening, Adella had a date with a most handsome young merman and she was having trouble deciding what to wear.

"Should I wear the green or the pink?" she asked her sisters. "Both look divine on me; it's so hard to choose."

"Oh, brother," said Ariel.

Adella turned to the mirror. She held her hair up, then let it down. Up. Down. Up. Down. "Which do you think is more stunning?" she asked.

"For heaven's sake, Adella!" said Aquata.

Adella opened her jewel box. She looked through it and held up a pearl necklace. "Well, I'm sick of this old thing," she said. "Have any of you got a *pink* pearl?"

"A pink pearl!" said Attina. "Oh, Adella, you know how impossible it is to find one of those."

"But I *want* one!" Adella insisted. "And I always get what I want!" And with that, she swam away.

"Someday Adella's vanity will make her go too far," said Ariel. Her sisters nodded in agreement.

Adella headed for the twisting dark caverns that led to oyster beds hardly ever visited by anyone in the kingdom. She thought she'd have more of a chance of finding a pink pearl if she went where other merpeople wouldn't

go. What she had forgotten was how dark and deserted a place she was entering.

She shrugged off her fear. I'm a princess, after all, she thought. What harm could possibly come to me?

Finally Adella came to a clearing where she found an oyster bed. She traveled from one oyster to another, searching for her treasure. She scoffed at the dozens of white pearls she passed. These are for ordinary merpeople, she thought.

She came, at last, upon an oyster with a perfect pink pearl nestled in its velvety center.

Adella stared at the pearl. It was magnificent, worthy of her. She began to talk to herself out loud about how wonderful the pearl would look in her hair that night, how this date would surely fall in love with her as quickly as had all her previous dates, how there was no one who would look as beautiful as she, and so on.

She did not notice that as she spoke, one by one the oysters closed their shells and seemed to sleep. Finally she reached in to take her pearl and go. Just then, the oyster let out a great snore and closed its shell, trapping Adella by the wrist.

"Hey!" she cried in surprise. "Let me go!"

But the ugly brown oyster did not budge.

"Pleeease let me go," she said, making her voice as sweet as she could.

Still the oyster did not budge.

Adella looked around. She was alone, surrounded only by bumpy oysters. Shadows seemed to be moving in the dark, cold water. And worst of all, no one really knew where she was. Adella began to get scared. She continued to talk, this time not quite so confidently.

"Did you hear that I'm a princess?" she asked the oyster. "My father is King Triton, and I am the most beautiful of his seven daughters. Wouldn't you like to help someone as important as I?"

The oyster snored loudly.

"I said," wheedled Adella, her voice getting a little higher, "wouldn't you be honored to free the most beautiful daughter of King Triton?"

But the oyster didn't move.

Finally Adella lost her temper.

"Open up, you ugly, slimy thing! How dare you hold me this way, you beastly, smelly creature! I deserve that pearl more than you do! I'm beautiful and graceful and a princess besides! You're just an icky, mossy shell!" she shrieked, pounding her fist on the top of the oyster and swishing her tail furiously.

But there was no response. Adella slumped down beside the oyster. How would she ever be found in time for her date, in time for her to do her hair and find the perfect outfit?

As Adella sat quietly, the oysters around her slowly began to open their shells. She looked hopefully at the oyster that held her. Slowly, slowly, it opened its shell, too, freeing Adella's wrist.

"Well, it's about time," said Adella. "You obviously don't realize who you are dealing with—"

"On the contrary," interrupted the oyster. "I know very well who I'm dealing with. A spoiled, vain princess who puts us all to sleep with her tiresome talk about herself. And I'm warning you, if you keep it up, I'm very likely to fall asleep again with my pearl inside me. So, little princess, if you want the pearl, take it, but be quiet and go!"

Adella had never had anyone speak to her this way. She was truly speechless, but she grabbed the pearl and began to swim away. Then she stopped, turned back, and carefully placed the pearl back where she had found it.

"You know, you've already given me a pearl," she said, "a pearl of wisdom, that I hope I will carry with me longer than I might have worn your pink pearl. Thank you." She ducked her head and swam off, eager to get ready for her date—with her old pearl necklace, which suddenly seemed quite lovely to her after all.

Fishy Holiday

Come one, come all,
In lake and pond,
In rivers flowing,
And beyond.
Little fishies come and play,
It's a splishy-splashy day!

Crystal streams,
And oceans deep,
Wake up fishies!
Do not sleep!
All the fishies shout "Hurray!"
It's a Fishy Holiday!

FISH
SCHOOL
CLOSED

A FISH OUT OF WATER

One day Flounder was busy playing with his friends when they began to talk about how far they had swum.

"Once I swam all the way to the underwater volcano!" said Swishy.

"Oh, that's nothing," boasted Fantail. "I do that all the time."

"Well, just yesterday I swam all the way to the coral reef and back!" gloated Snorkel.

One by one the fish tried to top each other in their tales of far-flung adventures. All except Flounder, that is. He was thinking how nice it was right here, in this little part of the sea, with its familiar places, his fish friends, Ariel and her sisters, and even crusty old Sebastian. He really didn't want to travel anywhere very far away. He liked home. But before he could think of how to explain this to his friends—SWOOSH!—he felt himself being scooped up out of the water and carried high above the sea. Flounder was in the beak of a big pelican!

"Hey!" he shouted as loudly as he could. "Put me down! Put me down!" But when he looked over the side of the pelican's beak, he was glad the bird was ignoring him. It looked like a looong way down. Finally the big bird flew down, down, down, and—PLOP!—Flounder was dropped into a little tidal pool.

The water felt so good on Flounder's scales that he splashed around happily for a few minutes while the pelican just watched him. Then he turned to the big bird and said, "Say, what's the big idea?"

But all the pelican said was, "I'm sorry if I've inconvenienced you, but now I've got to find my babies." And with a loud flap of her wings, she

was back in the air, soaring higher and higher.

"Take me home!" yelled Flounder, but he knew the pelican couldn't hear him. "What in the world could she want with me?" Flounder wondered. He decided he would ask Scuttle what birds want with fish when he got back home.

Swimming around in the tidal pool was lonely and boring. Flounder was glad when he heard voices coming, but when he looked up he gasped.

Humans! There were two little boys looking right down at Flounder!

All Flounder could think about were the terrible things he had heard about humans from everyone under the sea. Everyone, of course, but Ariel. During the hours Ariel and Flounder spent in her grotto with all her man-made treasures, Ariel spoke to Flounder about her hopes and dreams about human beings.

Flounder forced himself to think about the things Ariel had said. He smiled hopefully up at the two boys.

"Let's take him with us," said one boy to the other. And he leaned forward and scooped Flounder up in a pail.

Flounder tried not to be scared. He kept thinking that if Ariel liked humans, well, they couldn't all be that bad. He just wished he could go back home.

"Time to go, boys!" Flounder heard a voice call. "Hooray," he thought. "Now the boys will put me back in the ocean and I'll swim back to my friends."

But Flounder never heard the wonderful splash of his hitting the water. Instead he felt a thud. The boys had emptied the pail right on the street. And now they were pushing him down a hole.

"This is terrible!" said Flounder. "How will I get back to the sea now?"

SPLASH! Flounder opened his eyes. He was back in the water! It was a dark, narrow waterway, but it was water.

"I hope this is a good sign!" sighed Flounder.

He swam this way and that, looking for a way back to the sea. He raised his head above the water to have a look around and found himself face to face with a little gray mouse.

"Oh, please don't hurt me!" he begged when he saw the mouse's sharp white teeth.

"Calm down," said the mouse. "I'm not going to hurt you! I live down here."

"Really?" said Flounder. "Do you know which way I go to find the sea?"

"Go straight down this way and make a left. You'll know you're almost there when the water gets salty," the mouse said.

Flounder thanked the mouse and swam off as quickly as he could. When he could taste and smell the salty water, he swam even faster. He was too excited to be going home to even think he was tired.

"Flounder, you're safe!" Minnow cried when he saw his friend. "What happened? Where have you been?" Flounder told everyone the whole story.

"Humans," said Swishy. "You were with humans."

"Land," said Fantail. "You've been on land."

They all looked at their friend with deep respect. All their long swims could not compare with Flounder's dangerous journey.

"What a story this will make to tell your grandchildren!" said Snorkel.

Flounder just smiled. He wasn't sure he'd want to remember this day. It had been too full of adventure for his taste. He knew that one day he would be more than happy to tell his grandchildren about his friends and his adventures under the sea, where he belonged. But for right now, this tired little fish wanted a nice, long nap!

SCUTTLE'S UNDERWATER ADVENTURE

Ariel had just spent a very pleasant afternoon on the surface with Scuttle. She had found two more man-made objects for her collection and asked her seagull friend to identify them.

"This one here is a whatchamightcallit, and this other one, why it's a howdydoodle!"

Ariel sighed. "Scuttle, you know everything about humans. How do you do it?"

"It's simple, Princess," answered Scuttle, holding up a wing. "You can do whatever you put your mind to, you know." He slipped off his rock, but before he landed in the water, Ariel pushed him back up.

"I hope you're right, Scuttle," said Ariel, "because I have a mind to do a lot of things. But now I have to go." And with a quick peck on his beak and a little splash, Ariel was gone.

"So long, Princess," said Scuttle, and he looked around. This was always happening. His friends were always going back under the sea. Of course, that's where they lived, but a seagull could get lonely when his friends were fish and mermaids.

Gee, I'd like to know what goes on down there, thought Scuttle. "What was that I just told Ariel—brush after every meal? No. Neither a borrower nor a lender be? No, no, that's not it." Scuttle wrinkled his brow.

"I've got it!" he squawked, and almost slipped off his rock again. "You can do whatever you put your mind to." He nodded, pleased at his excellent memory.

"Now, why did I think that up again?" He scratched his head.

"Oh, yeah. I'd like to go under the sea and visit Ariel, and maybe if I close my eyes and put my mind to it, I can get there."

Scuttle squeezed his eyes shut. Sure is dark in here, he thought.

Scuttle thought and thought about what it must be like under the sea. He started to picture life under the water....

"Scuttle, what are you doing here?" asked Ariel in amazement.

Scuttle opened his eyes to find himself under the sea!

"I, er, I put my mind to it to see what it would be like to live under the ocean...so, er, here I am," said Scuttle, who was very pleased with himself and more than a little surprised.

Scuttle was having no trouble breathing. He was having no trouble seeing, either, thanks to the goggles he had brought along. He decided to try swimming. He used his wings as fins and his feet as flippers, but he had a hard time doing both at once.

"Swimming is pretty difficult," Scuttle mumbled.

Ariel thought Scuttle looked very funny, but she tried not to laugh. "You'll get the hang of it," she said. "Let's go find Flounder."

"Scuttle!" shouted Flounder when he saw his friends. "This is amazing. Wow, you're just like a fish—a birdfish!"

"Come with us, little buddy," Scuttle said to Flounder. "Ariel is going to show me around."

So the three friends went on their way. Scuttle was having trouble swimming, but he kept going. His eyes were wide open in wonder. How beautiful everything was!

"Ariel," he said, "there are more colors down here than on all the boats we've watched put together!"

Scuttle, Ariel, and Flounder swam to a coral reef where they played for a while. Scuttle picked up a large pink-and-white shell and held it to his ear. "I can hear the ocean," he said with a look of wonder. Ariel and Flounder giggled.

Next they swam past the palace and its gardens. "Nice little house you have there, Princess." Scuttle whistled in awe as they swam by.

As they passed the royal stables, Ariel asked, "Are you tired, Scuttle? Do you want to ride a seahorse?"

"Thank you, but no, Princess," said Scuttle. "I might get seasick! As a matter of fact, my wings are kind of pooped. I think I'll rest on this rock for a minute."

Ariel and Flounder went to swim nearby.

Suddenly, Scuttle sat straight up. It felt like his rock was moving.

"Oh, boy! I think I need some help here!" cried Scuttle.

Suddenly Scuttle *was* moving, and very fast. He wasn't on a rock at all—he was on a whale!

"Swim off, Scuttle! Swim off!" cried Ariel, but her friend was too scared. He held on to the whale's back and closed his eyes. The whale didn't know he was carrying a passenger and he went at top speed through the coral and seaweed. Scuttle's whole body shook up and down, and then he lost his grip. Forgetting he could swim, he slipped off the whale's back and landed on the ocean floor. He had a long way to swim back to his friends.

"Princess," said Scuttle when he reached them, "it's been great to visit you here, but I'm waterlogged. I've got to get back to my little island and dry out. See you."

Scuttle summoned the rest of his strength and swam upward. He climbed onto his rock, and back in the warm sun, he fell asleep instantly.

When he awoke the next morning, Scuttle stretched and yawned and said, "Boy, what a strange dream I had." Then he looked down and saw a strand of seaweed wound around his foot. "It was a dream, wasn't it?" And Scuttle put his mind to asking Ariel as soon as he saw her.

Sebastian's Frustration

As King Triton's court musician,
I write music on commission,
So we'll play a composition
Of my own.

I must ask you to be seated,
For King Triton has decreed it,
And just once I will repeat it—
Please sit down!

Yes, I see you're all excited,
And I'm sure that I'll be knighted,
For the king will be delighted
When we play.

What, your xylophone needs tuning?
And the bassoonists are all swooning?
And the tuna fish is crooning?
Why today?

Though this royal occupation
Is a life full of frustration,
To be Number One Crustacean
I persist.

So, please no more be delayers,
You're King Triton's famous players!
Oh, I don't know what the use is—
You're dismissed!

SEBASTIAN'S NEW OVERCOAT

"Hmmm," said Sebastian, staring into his closet. "What can I wear for the concert tonight? We are playing so many new pieces I do believe a new shell overcoat is in order."

Sebastian went out and began to look carefully at the ocean floor.

"It must be dignified," he said, "but with a little flair." Just then a shell caught his eye. "Why, the ladies will all swoon when they see me in this," he said, chuckling to himself. It was a very fine shell indeed—shiny pink on the outside, creamy white on the inside.

Sebastian tried it on. It fit splendidly over his own shell.

As Sebastian walked home, he began to hear a roaring sound. It felt as if the sound were all around him. Sebastian looked around, but he could see nothing. Then he saw Ariel and Flounder picking sea anemones.

Sebastian stopped and called to the princess. "Are you making that dreadful noise?"

Ariel looked up. "What noise?" she asked.

"Why, that rushing sound," said Sebastian. "It's…it's…why, it's stopped. How do you like my new overcoat for tonight's concert, Princess?" As Sebastian turned to model his new shell for Ariel, the noise began again. He stopped. The noise stopped. He turned. The noise came back. He stopped again. No noise.

"What a crazy coat!" cried Sebastian as he quickly took off the shell and tossed it down.

Ariel and Flounder laughed. "I guess when you move, the water passing through the shell makes a noise!" said Ariel.

"Shh, Princess, don't talk so loud. I have a headache! I will see you at the concert tonight." And Sebastian hobbled off, holding one claw to the side of his head. Before long, Sebastian came upon a beautiful, coiled snail shell. "This is more like it!" he said, wiggling into the shell. "Okay, ladies, come and get me!" he shouted. Sebastian began to strut and fell flat on his face!

"This is just a bit too tight!" he gasped, and squeeeezed himself out of the shell. "It won't do at all!"

Just then Alana and her turtle swam by. The turtle snatched up the shell, played with it for a moment, then crunched into it, shattering it to bits.

Sebastian was relieved indeed that he was no longer wearing the shell. He waved to Alana and the turtle and on he went.

Sebastian peered behind seaweed and under rocks, looking for a shell overcoat to wear to the concert that night. Then, almost hidden from sight, he spied something red and purple with bright yellow dots.

"Perfect!" Sebastian cried happily, and he pulled the large shell over his head.

"Very distinctive," he said, and twirled around. "No noise and quite a comfortable fit."

Sebastian smiled. He danced a little jig. He pretended to tip his hat. He bowed. He might have gone on like that for quite a while if he hadn't heard a noise behind him. He turned and saw Aquata, Arista, Andrina, Attina, and Adella covering their mouths with their hands as they howled with laughter.

"And just what is so funny?" Sebastian demanded, trying to hide his embarrassment at having been caught admiring himself.

"Sebastian," said Andrina, as gently as she could, "don't you think that overcoat is a bit too, well, *showy?*"

"The show!" cried Sebastian, "I must get to rehearsal!" He jumped out of the shell and began to hurry off. He looked back at the princesses.

"Ah…thank you," he said curtly, and was off.

"I guess I will have to conduct without an overcoat at all," said Sebastian. "There is just no more time to look for a new one and my old ones simply won't do."

At the end of the performance that night, everyone stood and clapped and clapped. King Triton made a special announcement.

"Sebastian, for all your excellent new music," he said, "I present you with this small token of my esteem." King Triton handed Sebastian a beautifully wrapped box. Inside was a brand-new, golden shell overcoat.

"Your Majesty!" Sebastian gasped. "How did you know that this is absolutely the very thing that I wanted most?" And while Sebastian tried on his new shell, which fit him just perfectly, seven little mermaids exchanged a pleasant wink with their father.

URSULA'S REVENGE

Under the sea there were ripples of excitement as the kingdom prepared to celebrate its biggest holiday. It was the anniversary of the day that King Triton had freed the kingdom from Ursula the Sea Witch. Everyone eagerly awaited the festivities that would mark this most special of days. Everyone, that is, except Ursula and her slimy eels, Flotsam and Jetsam.

Flotsam and Jetsam leaned over the crystal ball. "Hissss," they both said together.

"I'll win back the kingdom someday, and when I do, we'll just see how happy they'll all be then!" Ursula vowed. "But in the meantime, I've got to find a way to *really* make this a day to remember!"

Ursula looked in the crystal ball. She saw extra guards posted around the kingdom.

"They must be waiting for me to try something," said Ursula. "Disappoint them, I won't!" Quickly, she flipped through her *Book of Spells*. She stopped and read one page carefully.

"That's it!" she shrieked. "Why send only one Ursula to ruin things if you can send one hundred? Ursula, old girl, you've still got it!" Ursula rubbed her hands together gleefully and quickly began to mix a magic potion.

"Barnacle flakes, one squid tentacle, jellyfish venom," Ursula muttered as she dropped the ingredients into the pot. "One shark tooth, and—this has to be just right—a dash of barracuda juice!"

Smoky clouds began to billow from the pot. Black bubbles rose and burst. Ursula chuckled. She dipped her ladle into the pot and gulped

down the mixture. When she began to chuckle again, black bubbles rose out of her mouth. Inside each one was a tiny Ursula!

One hundred little black bubbles in all came out of Ursula's mouth. One hundred little Ursulas floated high above the sea's floor. The bubbles rolled out of the cave, off toward the kingdom.

"Hurry, my darlings!" Ursula cried. "Your bubbles will open for only a few minutes, so you must already be in the kingdom, ready to pinch, pilfer, and do whatever you can to ruin this sappy celebration! I know you can do it! Make me proud!"

Ursula waved to the bubbles as they danced off, rising higher and higher in the water.

One hundred bubbles floated right past the palace guards, high above their heads. The guards were peering anxiously into the distance, on the lookout for one big Ursula. They never thought to turn their eyes upward.

Ursula's spell seemed to be working perfectly. The bubbles burst inside the kingdom, as planned. One hundred tiny Ursulas giggled wickedly and set out to make as much mischief as they could in a hurry.

But just as they spread out to rip down decorations, overturn tables of food, pull merpeople's hair, and do many other equally nasty things, the annual beauty contest was announced. Each little Ursula immediately decided to enter the pageant. Back in her cave, Ursula watched through her crystal ball as her hundred little selves abandoned her plan.

"No! You vain little fools!" she cried as she pulled her hair. Ursula leaned closer as a trumpet blast signaled the beginning of the event. One of King Triton's heralds swished forward, cleared his throat, and announced:

"Ladies and gentlemen! I am honored to present the most beautiful and talented creatures under the sea!"

One by one the loveliest creatures in the kingdom came down the swimway. Each of King Triton's daughters performed well and never looked more beautiful. The judges exchanged glances. It would be difficult to pick just one winner.

Then, all of a sudden, one hundred little Ursulas, each one jealous of ninety-nine others, came down the swimway, kicking and screaming at each other. They pulled each other's hair. They kicked sand. They called each other terrible names.

All the mermaids and mermen crowded around as the fight raged on and on. No one knew what to do. Then a strange thing began to happen. Shiny black bubbles formed around each of the little Ursulas. They floated up past the castle, higher and higher. All the merpeople heard one hundred angry shrieks. Then the miniature witches floated away.

Ursula stopped looking into the crystal ball. She sat back and groaned. The one hundred black bubbles bobbed back into her cave. Ursula waited for them to vanish, but when the bubbles popped again, the little Ursulas inside did not disappear. Instead they kept on fighting.

"I must have used too much barracuda juice!" screamed the original Ursula. "What a day to remember this turned out to be after all!" she shrieked, and ran off to find her book of antidotes.

Ursula's Fury

That little brat!
That awful child!
I hear her voice
And just go wild!

To think that *she's*
So young and rich!
While look at me—
An old Sea Witch!

The way I'm treated
Is a sin!
But I'll fix her,
I'll do her in!

Oh, I love it!
I can't wait!
To make a poison
Of my hate!

MARLON'S
AMAZING DISCOVERY

One day Ariel, Flounder, and Ariel's cousin Marlon decided to play hide-and-seek in an old sunken ship half-buried in the ocean floor. Flounder was "It," so Ariel and Marlon swam quickly through the rotting planks looking for good places to hide.

Marlon went to the front of the ship and was about to hide in a big steamer trunk, when he noticed a strange shape in the murky water. He reached over and pulled away some seaweed that covered the object.

"Ariel, Flounder, come take a look at this!" Marlon shouted excitedly.

"What is it?" Ariel asked. Marlon pointed to his discovery.

"Oh!" Ariel and Flounder cried together. For there, carved in the prow of the ship, was the face of a young girl.

"It's a human figure, carved out of wood," said Ariel, tugging away more of the seaweed. "She's part of the ship."

Indeed, the wooden girl leaned forward from the front end of the ship. Her arms were crossed against her body, and her carved hair flowed back from her face.

"Let's clean her up," said Ariel. "Then we'll be able to see what she really looks like." And with that, she began to rub away the barnacles and moss that covered the girl's face and dress.

Every day Ariel returned to the ship to clean up the wooden girl. On the first day, Marlon went with her and helped Ariel brush the mud from the girl's eyes. On the second day, Flounder watched as Ariel scraped mud from the girl's hair. On the third day, Ariel scrubbed moss from her dress. On the fourth day, the girl was missing! Ariel gasped and looked

around wildly. Where could she be?

"Up here!" called a voice.

Ariel looked up. There, perched on the ship's mast, was a beautiful mermaid.

"Don't you recognize me?" the mermaid asked.

Ariel looked at the mermaid closely. Why, she looked just like the wooden girl from the ship!

"Let me explain," said the mermaid. "My name is Kate. I was a human girl. My father was a sea captain, and I loved to sail with him. One day I saw a handsome merman swimming in the water and I fell in love with him instantly. I could not stop thinking of him and longed to be by his side. It all seemed hopeless until a strange creature came to see me. Her name was Ursula."

"The Sea Witch!" Ariel cried. "She usually makes mischief *under* the sea. She must have been awfully bored below to work her evil on the surface."

"I don't know if she was bored," said Kate, "but I do know she was mean! She told me she knew of a magic spell that would change me into a mermaid three days after I saw my merman again. I wanted so badly to be with him that I didn't think to ask what the details were. I quickly agreed, and with an evil laugh Ursula changed me into a figure on the prow of my father's ship. She told me that this way I could keep a constant watch for my love."

"Ursula is usually more than just mean," said Ariel. "She usually wants something, too."

"Well, I never found out what it was," said Kate, "because that very night, there was a terrible storm that sank the ship."

"And you've been stuck here ever since," added Ariel.

"That's right," said Kate. Then she swam a little and stretched her arms over her head. "But thanks to you, I can see again! You brushed the mud away from my eyes."

"And you're a mermaid!" said Ariel excitedly. "You must have seen your merman!"

"I have," said Kate. "He's your cousin Marlon!" She gave Ariel a hug. "Will you take me to him?"

"Of course!" Ariel said, laughing. "But you must promise to tell me what it was like to be a human and to live on land."

"It's a deal," said Kate. "As soon as I've seen Marlon, I'll be happy to tell you anything you'd like to know."

Ariel couldn't wait to hear Kate's stories about life on land. She thought to herself that she could not imagine ever being so much in love that she would stoop to asking Ursula for help. But Kate could not possibly have known about Ursula and her evil tricks. And everything had turned out okay, or would, Ariel thought, as soon as Marlon saw the beautiful mermaid who longed to be with him. Ariel returned Kate's hug, and then the two mermaids linked arms and swam off together.

A DAY IN THE
LIFE OF A MERMAID

"Just look at that girl," Sebastian said, "loafing about, day-dreaming. Ariel, sometimes I think you've got seagrass for brains."

Ariel didn't even look up. She was busy doodling in the sand. She was thinking about humans. Humans had created so many wonderful things that she had found on the ocean floor. And humans lived on the surface. Ariel closed her eyes and began to remember all the stories she had heard from Kate, Scuttle, and the others about those strange creatures with legs instead of fins.

"Waah! Waah! Waaaaah!"

The crying interrupted Ariel's thoughts. She saw a little shrimp crying.

"What's the matter?" she asked. "Are you lost?"

The tiny shrimp nodded.

"Waah! Waah! Waah!"

"Okay, okay," Ariel said, lifting him up. "Don't you belong at Crayfish School?" She carried the little fellow carefully to the school, where he happily joined the other little shrimps.

Ariel watched as the little shrimps played, but soon she was thinking about life on land again. She wondered if humans went to school.

"Hey, Ariel! Want to dance?"

Ariel looked over her shoulder. There was Briny, with his eight left feet! Ariel groaned to herself. Briny was such a bad dancer! If only he knew that, but Ariel would never tell him. She just couldn't hurt his feelings.

"Please, Ariel?" Briny begged. "You can use some of my feet."

Sighing, Ariel held out her arms and let Briny lead her around. He twirled her and lifted her up until she got very dizzy.

"I think we'd better stop now," she said, after he had dipped her for the fifth time.

"Oh, sure, sure. Thanks a lot, Ariel. With a little practice you'll probably be a pretty good dancer someday," he said, waving good-bye with all eight legs.

Ariel was wondering what it would be like to dance with a human, when she heard a soft mewing nearby.

"What in the great green ocean," Ariel said. She looked around. There was her sister's pet catfish, Fin-Fin, all tangled up in a coral bed.

"How did you ever get out here?" she said as she carefully pulled Fin-Fin out of the coral bed. "Attina doesn't like for you to get out of the castle." The catfish purred in Ariel's arms, and they swam back to the castle side by side.

As soon as Ariel arrived at the castle, Adella whisked her away to their bedroom.

"Ariel," she said excitedly. "I need to ask you a favor. Will you lend me your mother-of-pearl comb? I've got a big date tonight, and it will look divine in my hair."

Ariel found the comb in her jewel box, but of course Adella wanted her to arrange her hair for her as well.

"You're so clever with hair, Ariel," Adella said, patting her hair in place. "It's a shame you just let yours go." Then she blew Ariel a kiss and floated out the door.

"Hmmm," Ariel thought, peering at her reflection. She piled all her hair on top of her head. Then she let it drop again. "I wonder if humans wear their hair up or down."

She was about to try a braid when Arista burst in.

"Ariel, come quickly!" Arista pleaded. "It's Mackey's day off and someone left the stable door open. Foamy's loose!"

Ariel swam out to the stables, where she and Arista finally cornered Foamy and led him back to his stall.

"Thanks for your help," Arista said as she closed the stable door tightly.

"Do you think humans have any animals like seahorses?" Ariel wondered.

"Are you kidding?" Arista scoffed. "They have to get around on their ugly old legs."

"I don't think legs are ugly at all," said Ariel. "Haven't you ever thought about what it must be like to walk on land?"

"Ariel!" said Arista, shocked. "Why would you want to walk on land when you can swim in the ocean?"

Ariel could not give her sister a simple answer so she swam off without answering and went back to her doodles. She began to daydream about walking on land. Everyone would marvel at how graceful she was and beg her to dance, and, and—

But Ariel never finished her thought. She was interrupted by Sebastian.

"Look at that girl," he complained. "She hasn't moved from that spot all day."

Ariel just looked at Sebastian and smiled.

Ariel's Dream

I've always tried so hard to be
What everyone expects of me.
But lately I've a nagging thought
That goes against all I've been taught.

The world above seems bright and wide,
And yet, down here is where we hide.
There's something that just isn't right
With living here without sunlight.

For now I'll dream among the waves
And keep collections in my caves.
I know there has to be a way
That I can live on land one day.